They Never Told Me

They Never Told Me

AND OTHER STORIES

AUSTIN CLARKE

EXILE
editions

Library and Archives Canada Cataloguing in Publication

Clarke, Austin, 1934-, author
    They never told me : and other stories / Austin Clarke.

Short stories.
ISBN 978-1-55096-359-5 (pbk.)

    I. Title.

PS8505.L38T48 2013   C813'.54   C2013-905116-3

Design and Composition by Mishi Uroboros
Cover Art by Luke Siemens
Typeset in Fairfield, Trajan and Constantia fonts at Moons of Jupiter Studios

Published by Exile Editions Ltd ~ www.ExileEditions.com
144483 Southgate Road 14 – GD, Holstein, Ontario, N0G 2A0
Printed and Bound in Canada in 2013, by Imprimerie Gauvin

We gratefully acknowledge, for their support toward our publishing
activities, the Canada Council for the Arts, the Government of Canada
through the Canada Book Fund (CBF), the Ontario Arts Council, and
the Ontario Media Development Corporation.

Canadian Sales: The Canadian Manda Group, 165 Dufferin Street,
Toronto ON M6K 3H6 www.mandagroup.com 416 516 0911

North American and International Distribution, and U.S. Sales:
Independent Publishers Group, 814 North Franklin Street,
Chicago IL 60610 www.ipgbook.com toll free: 1 800 888 4741

for
Es'kia Mphahlele

Galaxie

After the twenty-nine years he born and living in Barbados, drunk as Calvin was, he saying, "Well, I won't be
see you for a while, man, I going up." Canada now gone
straight to his head long time and with a king o' power,
so that when the airplane start up Calvin imagine that he
own the whole blasted plane along with the white ladies
who tell him, "Good morning, sir"; he feel that the plane
is the big motorcar he intent to own one year after he
land pon Canadian soil. The plane making time fast fast,
and Calvin drink rum after rum till he went fast asleep
and didn't even know he was in Toronto. The white lady
come close to him, and tap him soft soft pon his new
tropical suit and say, "Sir?" like she is asking some important question, when all she want is to wake up Calvin
outta the white man plane. Well, Calvin wake up. He
stretch like how he uses to stretch when he wake up in
his mother bed. He yawn so hard that the white lady
move back a step or two, after she see the pink inside his
mouth and the black and blue gums running all round
them white pearly teets. Calvin eyes red red as a cherry
from lack o' sleep and too much rum drinking, and the
body tired like how it uses to get tired and wrap up like

a old motorcar fender. But is Canada, old man, and in a jiffy, before the white lady get to the front o' the place to put down the last glass, Calvin looking out through the window. "Toronto in your arse!" he went to say to himself, but it come out too loud, "Toronto in your arse, man!"

Before the first week come and gone, Calvin take up pen and paper:... *and I am going to tell you something, this place is the greatest place for a workingman to live. I hear some things about this place, but I isn't a man to complain, because while I know I am a man, and I won't take no shit from no Canadian, white, black, or red, I still have another piece of knowledge which says that I didn't born here. So I controls myself to suit, and make the white man money. The car only a couple of months off. I see one already that I got my eyes on. And if God willing, by the next two months I sitting down in the driver's seat. The car I got my eyes on is a red one with white tires. The steering wheel as you know on the left side, and we drives on the right-hand side of the road up here, not like back in Barbados where you drive on the left-hand. Next week, I taking out my licence. I not found a church I like yet, mainly because I see some strange things happening up here in church. You don't know, man, but black people can't or don't go in the same church as white people. God must be have two colours then. One for black people and one for white people. And a next thing. There is some fellas up here from the islands who talking a lot of shit about*

Black Power. I am here working for a living and a motor-car and if my mother herself come in my way and be an obstacle against me getting them two things, a living and a motorcar, I would kill her by Christ... Calvin was going to write more; about the room he was renting for twenty dollars a week, which a white fellow tell him was pure robbery, because he was paying ten dollars for a more larger room on the ground floor in the same house; and he didn't write bout the car-wash job he got the next day down Spadina Avenue, working for a dollar a hour, and when the first three hours pass he felt he been working for three days, the work was so hard; he didn't tell that a certain kind of white people in Canada didn't sit too close to him on the streetcar, that they didn't speak to him on the street... lots o' things he didn't worry to tell... so Calvin work hard, man, Calvin work more harder than when he was washing off cars back in Barbados. The money was good too. Sal'ry and tips. From the two car-wash jobs he uses to clear a hundred dollars a week, and that is two hundred back home, and not even Dipper does make that kind o' money, and he is the fucking prime minister! The third job, Calvin land like a dream: night watchman with a big big important company which put him in big big important uniform and thing, big leather belt like what he uses to envy the officers in the Volunteer Force back home wearing pon a Queen Birthday parade on the Garrison Savannah, shoes the company people even provide, and the only thing that was missing, according to what Calvin figure out some months afterwards, was that the holster at his side, join-on to the leather belt, didn't have in no blasted gun. He tell it to a next Barbadian he make friends with, and the Bajun just laugh and say, "They think you going rass-hole shoot yourself, boy!" But Calvin did already become Canadified enough to know that the only people he see in them uniforms with guns in the leather holster was certain white people, and he know he wasn't Canadified so much that he did turn white overnight. "Once it don't stop me from getting that Galaxie!"... he went down by the Tropics Club where they play calypsos and dance, one time, and he never went back cause the ugly Gren-adian fellow at the door ask him for "three dollars to come in!" and he curse the fellow and leff. But the bank account was mounting and climbing like a woman belly when she in the family way. Quick quick so, Calvin have a thousand dollars pon the bank. Fellas who get to know Calvin and who Calvin won't 'sociate with because 'soci-ating does cost money, boy!" Them fellas so who here donkey years, still borrowing money to help pay their rent, fellas gambling like hell, throwing dice every Fridee night right into Mondee morning early, missing work and getting fired from work, fellas playing poker and betting, "Forty dollars more for these two fours, in your rass, sah! I *raise*!" – them brand o' Trinidadian, Bajun, Jamaican,

Grenadian and thing, them so can't understand at all how Calvin just land and he get rich so fast. "I bet all-yuh Calvin selling pussy!" one fella say. A next bad-minded fella say, "He peddling his arse to white boys down Yonge Street," and a third fella who did just bet fifty dollars pon a pair o' deuces, and get broke at the poker game, say quick quick before the words fall out o' the other fella mouth, "I goint peddle mine too, then! Bread is bread."

Calvin start slacking up on the first car-wash work, and he humming as he shine the white people car, he skinning his teet in the shine and he smiling, and the white people thinking he smiling because he like the work and them, cause his hands never tarried whilst he was car-dreaming, they drop a little dollar bill pon Calvin as a tip, and a regular twenty-five-cent piece, and Calvin pinching pon the groceries, eating a lotta pigs feet and chicken necks and salt fish… all the time work work so that Calvin won't even spend thirty cents pon a beer with a sinner, an' the only time he even reading is when he clean out a car in the car wash and it happen to have a used paper inside it, or a throwaway paperback book. For Calvin decided long time that he didn't come here for eddication. He come for a living and a motorcar. And he intend to get both. And by the look o' things, be-Christ, both almost in his hand. Only now waiting to see the right model o' motorcar, with the right colour inside it, and the right mileage and thing. The motorcar must have the right colour o' tires, right colour o' gearshift and in the handle too. And it have to have-in radio; and he see a fella in the car wash with a thing inside his Cadillac, and Calvin gone crazy over Cadillacs until he walk down by Bay Street and price the price of a old one. He bawl for murder, "Better stick to the Galaxie, boy!" he tell himself; and he do that. But he really like the thing inside the white man Cadillac and he ask the man one morning what it was, and the man tell Calvin. Now Calvin must have red Galaxie, with not more than twenty-thousand miles on the register, black upholstery, red gearshift, radio, AM and FM and a tellyfone. Them last three things is what the man had inside his Cadillac. Calvin working even on a Syundee, bank holidays ain' touching Calvin, and the Old Queen back home who send a occasional letter asking Calvin to remember the house rent and the Poor Box in the Nazarene Church where he was a testifying brother, preaching and thing, and also to remember "who birthed him," well, Calvin tell the Old Queen, his own own mother, *Things hard up here, Mother. Don't let nobody fool you that because a man emigrade it mean that he elevate.*

Even so, a month and a half later, two days before Calvin decide he see the right automobile, a card drop through the door where Calvin living, address to Calvin: *What are you doing up there, then? Canadians buying out all the island. You standing for that? Send down a couple of dollars and let me invest it in a piece of beach land for you, Brother. Power to the people! Salaam and love. WILLY X.* Calvin get so blasted vex, so damn vex, cause he sure now that this Willy gone mad too, like everybody else he been reading bout in the States and in England; black people gone mad, Calvin say; and he get more vex when he think that it was the landlady, Mistress Silvermann, who take up the postcard from the linoleum and hand it to him, and he swear blind that she hand it to him after she done read the thing: and now she must be frighten like hell for Calvin, cause Calvin getting letters from these political extremists, and birds of a feather does flock together, she thinking now that Calvin perhaps is some kind o' political maniac, crying Black Power! All this damn foolishness bout Power to the People, and signing his name Willy X, when everybody in Barbados know that that damn fool's name is really William Fortesque: Calvin get shame shame shame that the landlady thinking different bout him, because sometimes she does be in the house alone all night with Calvin, and she must be even thinking bout giving him notice, which would be a damn bad thing to happen right now, cause the motorcar just two days off, the room he renting now is a nice one, the rent come down like the temperature in May when he talk plain to Mistress Silvermann bout how he paying twice as much as other tenants, but what really get Calvin really vex vex vex as hell is that a little Canadian thing in the room over his head come downstairs one night in a mini-dress and thing, bubbies jumping bout inside her bosom, free and thing and looking juicy, and giggling all the time and calling sheself a women liberation, all her skin at the door, and the legs nice and fat just as Calvin like his meats, and Calvin already gone thinking that this thing is the right woman to drive bout in his new automobile with, this Canadian thing coming downstairs every night for the past month, and out of the blue asking him, "You'll like a coffee?" When she say so the first time, coffee was as far from Calvin mind as lending Willy twenty-five cents for the down payment for the house spot pon the beach back home. Now, be-Christ, Willy X, or whatever the hell that bastard calling himself nowadays, is going to stay right there down in Barbados and mash up Calvin life so! Just so? Simple so? Oh, God, no, man! But the landlady couldn't read English, she did only uses to pretend she is a genius; but the Canadian girl is who tell Calvin not to worry; one night when they was drinking the regular coffee in the communal kitchen, the Canadian girl say, "Missis Silvermann is only a D.P. She can't read English." Calvin take courage. The bankbook walking bout with him, inside his trousers all the time, he counting the digits going to work, coming from work, in the back seat alone, pon the streetcar, while waiting for the subway early on a morning at the Ossington

Station, and then he make a plan. He plan it down to a T. Every penny organize for the proper thing, every nickel with its own work to do: the bottle of wine that the Canadian girl gave him the name to; the new suit from Eaton's that he see in the display window one night when he get hold of the girl and he get bold bold as hell and decide to take she for a lover's walk down Yonge Street; the new shoes, brown brown till they look red to match the car; and the shirt and tie – every blasted thing matching up like if he is a new bride stepping down the aisle to the wedding march. And he even have a surprise up his sleeve for the thing, too. He isn' longer a stingy man, cause he see his goal; and his goal is like gold. The car delivery arrange for three o'clock, Sardah; no work; the icebox in his room have in a beer or two, plus the wine; and he have a extra piece o' change in his pocket…
"I going have to remember to change the money from this pocket," he tell himself, as if he was talking to some-body else in the room with him, "to the next pocket in the new suit"… and he have Chinese food now on his mind because the Canadian thing mention a nice Chin-ese restaurant down in Chinatown near Elizabeth Street. Calvin nervous as arse all Fridee night; all Fridee night the thing in Calvin room (here of late she behaving as if she live in Calvin room), and Calvin is a man with ambi-tions: one night she tantalize Calvin head so much that he start talking bout high-rise apartment; perhaps, if she

behave sheself he might even put a little gold thing pon her pretty little pink finger… the girl start asking Calvin if he want some; not in them exact words, but that is what she did mean; and Calvin turn shame shame and nearly blush, only thing, as you know black people can't show really if they blushing or if they mad as shit with a white person, and Calvin turn like a virgin on the night before she getting hang in church and in marriage, and he saying all the time cause his mind pon the mileage in the motorcar, "Want some o' what?" And the girl laugh, and she throw back she head and show she gold fillings and she pink tongue and the little speck o' dirt under she neck; and she laugh and say to sheself, "This one is a real gentleman, not like what my girlfriend say to expect from West Indian men, at all…" And you know something? She start one big confessing: "…and do you know what, Calvin? Would you like to hear something that I been thinking…" Calvin thinking bout motorcar and this blasted white woman humbugging him bout sex! Calvin get vex, he play he get vex bout something different from the woman and she sex, and he send she flying back upstairs to she own room. He get in bed too, but he ain' sleeping, he wide awake in the dark like a thief, and he eyes open wide wide wide like a owl eyes, and in that darkness in that little little room that only have one small window way up by the ceiling and facing the clotheslines and the dingy sheets that the landlady does spend all week washing, Calvin see the whole o' Toronto standing up and watching him drive by in his new motorcar – with the Canadian thing beside o' him in the front seat! – dream turn into different dream that Fridee night, because he was free to dream as much as he like since Sardah wasn' no work. Sardah is car day. He have everything plan. Go for the motorcar, pick it up, drive it home, pick up the Canadian thing, go for a spin down Bloor as far as Yonge, swing back up by Harbord, turn left at Spadina, take in College Street, and every West Indian in Toronto bound to see him in new car, before he get back home. Park she in front o' the house, *let everybody see me getting outta she, come in, have a little bite, change, change into the new suit, given the Canadian thing the surprise, and whilst she dressing, I sit down in the car…* "And I hope she take a long time dressing so I would have to press the car horn, press the horn just a little, a soft little thing, and call she outside, to see me in the…" Morning break nice. It was a nice morning round the middle o' September, fall time in the air, everybody stretching and holding up their head cause the weather nice. Even the cops have a smile on their fissiogomy.

The salesman-man smile and shake Calvin hand strong, and give Calvin the history of the bird although Calvin did already hear the bird history before. The salesman-man come outta the office still smiling, holding the motorcar keys between the index finger and the big thumb, and he drop them in Calvin hand. Calvin make a shiver. A shiver o' pride and ownership. "Galaxie in your arse!" He say that in his mind, and he thinking o' Willy and the boys back in Marcus rum shop. He get in the car. He shuffle bout a bit in the leather seat. He straighten he trousers seams. He touch the leather. He start up the motor. Listen to the motor. It ticking over like a fucking charm. He put the thing in gear. And he bout to make a little thing through the car park, and he would have gone straight back up Danforth if the Canadian thing didn't wave she pocketbook to remind Calvin that she come with he, cause Calvin did forget she standing up there looking at a white convertible Cadillac, which she say is the car for Calvin, that there is lots o' "Negro-men driving them, even in Nova Scotia where I come from," that Calvin should have buy one o' them. "You start spending my blasted money already, woman! This is *mine*!" He didn't tell she out loud in words what he was really thinking bout she, but he was thinking so, though.

The Canadian she get in the motorcar, cause driving in a Galaxie more better than walking behind a Cadillac, and she sit down so comfortable that it look like if she own the car and she was giving Calvin a chance to try she out, and that it wasn't Calvin own own money that pay-down pon the car. Calvin didn't like that at all: he want she to sit down in the front seat like if he own the

motorcar. But Calvin gone up Danforth with new motorcar and white woman beside o' him, like if he going to a
funeral; "Got to break she in gently, man"; though the
horses under the bonnet roaring like hell. Well, they
drive and drive like if they was two explorers exploring
Toronto: through Rosedale where the Canadian thing say
she would just love to own a house; and in his mind,
Calvin promise she she going get one in Rosedale;
through the Bridle Path where she say the cheapest
house cost a million dollars; through Don Mills where
they see the big tall Foresters' Building, all up there by
IBM; "You should get a job at IBM, dear" ("Doing wha?
Cleaning out the closets?"... this Canadian thing like
she is the wrong kind o' woman for me. Calvin thinking:
I hads better get a black woman!); all this she talk as they
driving back on the Don Valley Parkway. The highway
nice. The motorcar open a new whole life to Calvin, and
he love Toronto even better. Damn good thing he leff
Barbados! The Galaxie like a horse, prancing pon the
white man road. Night fall long time as they travelling,
and Calvin experimenting with the dip-lights and the
high beam. It nice to play with. The FM radio thing ain't
working good cause Calvin never play one o' them radios
before, and he forget to practice pon it when he was visiting the car in the lot after he pay-down something pon
it, so that the salesman would keep it for him. So he
working the AM thing overtime. A nice tune come on.

Before the time come on, he thinking again that the Canadian thing may be the right woman for him: she nice, she tidy, and she quiet. And he raise-up liking quiet women; his mother tell him never marry a woman who ain' quiet, and like church. The tune is a calypso, man. "It's a nice calypso," Calvin say. "Sparrow, in your arse!" he shout, and he beg pardon, he excited because it is the first time he hear a calypso on the radio. He start liking Canada bad bad again. "Look at me, though! New car! A Galaxie, and you beside me..." The Canadian thing start working up she behind beside o' Calvin; she start saying she been going down in the islands for years now, that she have more calypso records than any white woman in Toronto, and she wish she had the money to take them outta storage and play one or two for Calvin. She start singing the tune, and Calvin vex as hell, cause he don't like no woman who does sing calypso, his Old Queen didn't even let him sing calypso when he was a boy in Barbados. And he was a man! Besides, the calypso that the Canadian thing singing now is a thing bout "...*three white women travelling through Africa!*" and something about "*Uh never had a white meat, yet!*" and this nice woman, this simple-looking Canadian girl know all the words, and she enjoying sheself too, and Calvin thinking that Sparrow watching him from through the AM radio thing, and laughing at him, and he vex as shit, cause the calypso mean that certain white women like black men to lash them, and… "Don't sing that!" he order the thing, as if he talking to his wife; and the Canadian thing tell him, in a sharp voice, that she isn't his damn wife, so "Don't you be uppity with me, buster!" Well, who tell she she could talk back to a Bajan man like Calvin? Calvin slam on the brakes. The motorcar cry out *screeennnnch-hhhhh*! The Canadian thing head hit the windshield, *bram*! And she neck like it break in truth. The motorcar halfway in the middle o' the highway. Traffics whizzing by, and the wind from them like it want to smash-up Calvin new Galaxie. Calvin vex as shit but he can't do nothing cause he trembling like hell: the woman in the front seat turning white white white like a piece o' paper, and the blood gone outta she face; Calvin ain' see no dimples in she face; and she ain' moving, she ain' talking, not a muscle ain' shiver. Traffics whizzing by and one come so damn close that Calvin close his eyes, and pray. "Look my blasted crosses! And my Galaxie ain' a fucking day old yet!" He try to start up the motor and the motor only coughing like it have consumption. The woman like she sleeping or dead or something. The calypso still blaring over the AM radio, and Calvin so jittery he can't find the right button to turn the blasted thing off. And sudden so, one of the traffics flying by is a police. Calvin hear, *weeeeeeeeeeeeeeeeeeeeeeennnnnnnnnnnnnnnnnnnnnnnn*! Sirens! A police car in the rear-view mirror. Calvin stop shaking sudden sudden. He start thinking. White woman deading in his new motorcar, the car new, and he is a stranger in Canada. He jump out and lift up the hood, and he back his new jacket, playing he is a mechanic. The police stop. He face red as a beet. "What's holding you up, boy!" Calvin hear the "boy," and he get vex, but he can't say nothing, cause they is two gainst his one, and he remember that he black. But he ain' no damn fool. He talk fast and sweet, and soft, and he impress the police:… "and Officer, I just now now give this lady a lift, she say she feeling bas, and I taking she to the hospital, cause as a West Indian I learn how to be a Good Samaritan, and…" The police ask for the licence, and when he see that the ownership papers say that Calvin only had the car this morning, the police, he smile, and say, "You are a Good Samaritan, wish our coloured people were more like you West Indians…" They lift the Canadian thing with she neck half-popped outta the Galaxie and into the cruiser, and Calvin even had a tear in his eye too. But the police take she away, and the siren start up again, *weeeeeennnnnnn*… Calvin manage to get the Galaxie outta the middle o' the road, the traffics still flying by, but now the new motorcar safe at the side o' the road. He put back on his jacket, and he shrug the jacket in shape and it fit pon his shoulders, he turn off the AM radio thing with the calypso, another calypso it was playing now, and fix the seams in his trousers, look back on the highway in the rear-view mirror, and start up the Galaxie. He driving slow slow on the highway and the traffics blowing their horn to tell him get the fuck outta the road, nigger, but all the time he smiling and holding his hand outta the window and waving them on. He outta habit bout to say something to the Canadian thing beside him, forgetting that she ain' there no more, and he still say, "This Galaxie is car for so! And godblummuh, look what a close shave I had!" He see the Canadian thing handbag open on the seat beside o' him, and he run his hand through it searching. It had in it five single dollar bills. He snap the handbag shut, touch the automatic window-winder, and throw the blasted handbag out the Don Valley Parkway, pon the road.

Waiting for the
Postman to Knock

That poor girl, Enid! The whole week Enid lay down in she bed, waiting for the postman to knock. The sheets and the blanket which the Jewish woman she was working for give she for Christmas last Christmas was wrap over she head, and she was in pain from head to foot. Enid wet her pillow, I tell you, with tears of blood. She had just been discharge from the General Hospital, but she was still weaky weaky and poorly. And not a dollar to her name! I ain't telling you no lie. This is a true, true story! Two times for the whole week she manage to get outta bed, to rub she arms and legs with some Canadian Healing Oil which she mother had send up for her last year. Enid was so sick that she was barely able to wash she face and hands. When she move in the bed the pain, child, the pain increase a little more. And water was coming outta Enid eyes like Niagara Falls self.

Winter, child, snow was outside like if somebody had paint the whole world white. And sadness dwelling inside Enid bedroom. Enid cry and cry and all the time she crying she cussing sheself that she ever was foolish enough to say she emigrading to the terrible place call Canada. Not a blind soul to make a cup o' tea or coffee for she; nobody to run to the corner store to buy a bottle of ginger ale, a pack o' chewing gum, not even mensing pads, then! Is so Enid lonely in this big country. You could imagine what it was for Enid, because even when she was strong and in good health she always uses to say how hard it is for a black woman living by sheself in this damn country. I hear with my own ears one day, as Enid curse God and Canada, and say, "Be-Jesus Christ, it isn't no bed of roses for a black woman living in this blasted country." Enid wait and wait for the postman to knock, and whilst she waiting, she decide to write a letter to the landlord. But the exertion nearly kill she. Anyhow, lissen to the letter Enid write:

46 Asquith Avenue
Toronto 5, Ontario
18 December

Dear Mr. Landlord,

I am a sick woman. I barely crept out of my room yesterday to go to the bank to see what happened to that cheque I wrote for you. Well, I can tell you, Mr. Landlord, that I don't understand how my money could disappear so fast from that Royal Bank. The woman behind the desk looked at my card, and she told me I have two dollars to my name. One dollar and eighty cents to be exact. I know I still owing you the rent, but I am not going to run, for as I say, I am a sick lady. I only told you that to tell you this. This morning before I even crawl out of bed, somebody was knocking down my door. I didn't even open my eyes yet, nor say a word to God for sparing my life at night. But I open the door. When I open the door, facing me is a man from Beneficial Finance Company of Canada. He come for cash. The next few minutes it is the postman. Registered letter. The Bell Telephone people start writing me threatening letters. I owe them nineteen dollars, nineteen stinking dollar and they hounding me as if I am a Mafia-woman. The Hydro people called up on the same phone and threaten me that they going cut off my electricity. I do my cooking by electricity, Mr. Landlord. I live by electricity. Electricity lights up this little room that I renting from you, when the nights come. If those Hydro people does cut off the electricity as they threaten to do, how am I going to see? And on top of all that, you now come telling me that I must vacate your premises? Well, Mr. Landlord, you listen to me now, sir. I am only telling you a few of the things that happens to black people in this country to let you know that it ain't no honeymoon living in this place. I came into this country as a decent middle-class person back in Barbados. I did not pay any racketeer to get me here illegal. And I did not come into this country on no underground railroad, neither. I came in legal. And I came in clean. And I came as a landed immigrant. It is written down on my passport. So I am saying this to you, to let you know that it is only in Canada that I am known as a labourer, or a working woman, as it is called in this country, because back home I never lifted a straw in the way of work, for my parents were rich people. We had servants back home. And if I wanted a glass of water, our maid brought it to me. I have spent the last five years up in Forest Hill working off my sweat for a lady by the name of Silverstein. And the sad thing is that I do not have anything today in my hour of sickness to show as a testimony to that hard work. So you can't treat me as if I am any D.P. person. I am a human being. And I am not writing this to you as if I do not like work. I know I have to work for my living in this country. But it is the conditions that I am talking about. And I want you to know too that I not writing this to you to beg you for nothing. I was not hiding from you, Mr. Landlord. I was not hoarding up my money in the Royal Bank, and telling you that I broke when you come for your rent. I was flat on my back in the Toronto General Hospital bed. Six weeks run into seven, and I was still there sprawled out in something called a semi-private. My temperature was all up in the hundreds, and I was roasted up night and day. All my savings I had to pay out in Blue Cross, Red Cross, PSI, doctor bills and I don't know what. So because of all these troubles that I face in your country, I am asking you now, as a human being, to let me live in this room a next month until I can get my hands on a piece of change. Somebody told me of a job up in Cooksville, which as you know is not close to Toronto, if you don't have a motorcar. And the moment I pacify these pains, I intend to go up to Cooksville. I am not a lazy person. I never was. Christmas is just round the corner. I have gifts to buy and send back home. And today, on this cold-winter-day, I do not even have a dime to buy a postcard with, to send for my mother for Christmas, in Barbados. And you come telling me about vacate?

Respectfully yours,
Miss Enid Scantlebury.

Child, that is the letter Enid write to the landlord-man. God, that girl have heart and she have guts to do a thing like that.

Well, the very next day, a special-delivery letter come back from the landlord-man. It say:

CROWN TRUST COMPANY, INC.
19 December
Miss E. Scantlebury
46 Asquith Avenue
Toronto 5, Ontario

Dear Miss Scantlebury,

We are in receipt of your most recent letter dated December 18. We regret to inform you that due to the heavy arrears of your rent, we find it impossible to extend your tenancy of the room at the above-mentioned address.

We urge you not to correspond further with us on this matter.

Yours faithfully,
(Signed) CROWN TRUST COMPANY, INC.
PS. Please note that our proper title is not "Mr. Landlord," but the Crown Trust Compoany, Inc., c/o Mortgage Department.

As you can expect, Enid gone mad now. Mad, mad, mad as hell! Everything turned out wrong, and the pain working now from in her shoulder blade all through her right side. And you know what women in the Wessindies does say when a young healthy woman start to get them kind o' pains! Enid tell me she start thinking bout home, bout Mammy, which is what she calls her mother, bout her boyfriend, and she sorry as hell that she didn't send for him when he did first ask to come up and married she. Well, thinking bout the devil, bram! a letter push under the door, from guess-who? Lonnie! Lonnie write to Enid and say how things back home really bad with him. Look, I going to read the whole letter, cause it is something to hear:

Haggatt Hall
Bridgetown
Barbados
The West Indies
16 December

Darling Sweetheart Enid,
This is Lonnie. I writing you because Christmas soon here, and things down here still rough rough with me in Barbados. The sugar cane crop season was a real bastard, and the estates been laying off men left and right like flies. Furthermore, a piece of sickness had me flat on my backside last month, and I had to give up the little picking a fellow by the name of Boulez from up in Christ Church parish had get for me. It was a real part-time job. I work for three days. Things real rough as I said, down here in this island, although we have independence and things like that. We have a Hilton hotel here as you know and

now people talking about building another big fancy hotel call the Holiday Inn. Both of them places build on Gravesend Beach where the sailors from the Boer War is buried. And where me and you used to go and bathe on a bank holiday and on Sunday mornings. Men walking about in Bridgetown like ants, unemploy. You have to be a craftsman to get a job these days. And as you know I am not no blasted craftsman, because I think that things like carpenters and masons is low jobs for a man in my position. Christmas soon come, and I would like to go to church five o'clock Christmas morning, at the Cathedral, because the news is that the new black bishop going to preach there. But I do not have my Christmas suit yet. The one I wear to the airport to wish you goodbye when you were leaving do not look good anymore. I buy a piece of cloth some time back, dark with a pin stripe, from Cave Shepherd store, about three months pass, when things was selling out. But Cuthbert the tailor fellow, since he come back down from up in the States and Northamerica and places like that, he now charging everybody a hell of a lot of money to make a suit and he adding on something he picked up up there in the States called "sales tax" and "luxuries tax." And nobody down here don't know what Cuthbert really mean by those two terms. But if you don't pay them, you can't touch your own suit when it finish made, if it made at all. So, darling love, Enid, I beseeching you, to please send a little something for me for Christmas. I want that suit bad bad out of Cuthbert hand, because I have not been near to a church since that Sunday when Trevour was christen.

Your loving man, Lonnie.

Child, there is a kind o' Wessindian man who just loves to live offa women. And Enid is such a kind-hearted person that she would give a sinner the dress offa her back. But Lonnie? Well, he is something else, a diff'rent story altogether!

Enid say she know now, long-time, Lonnie is the wrong man for she. Enid cry and cry and cry. She there flat on her back, trying to catch her strength and a man write her all the way from Barbados asking for money. When she read Lonnie letter, she tell me, she could only crawl outta her sickbed, stumble in the bathroom and look at her face in the mirror whilst she was crying. Child, you does read these things in certain magazines, but you *never never* think that life is really like this! Enid wipe her face and dust some powder on her face, and try to smile, cause it looked like whatever the hell she do, is only misery and sufferation coming her way.

Well, not that Enid didn' love Lonnie, at least once upon a time that was the case, as Enid tell me. But getting that letter from Lonnie, the man she had in mind to marry, threw her back, poor soul, right on another letter she had receive from Mammy some time back, before she went in the hospital. This is what Mammy write Enid, part of it:

I have received the few bills of money that you posted to me in March gone, this year. And I have been reposing myself down at the front window that you used to sit down at, and sing those lovely refrains you learned at the Fontabelle Christian Mission Church, waiting for the postman to ring his bicycle bell and then knock. Every time I see the postman pass across on his three-speed bicycle, my heart gives a leap and tears come to my eyes, because I know you have not send me anything. You have not remembered me. Nothing. Your own child, Trevour, have been sick every day for two weeks. Lonnie does not come around and even say, Take that, to the child, meaning common coins. All he does come round for is to ask, Enid send the thing? Child, you are my only child, but I have to tell you that I don't see the wisdom in you worrying out yourself behind a man like Lonnie. Lonnie not good. Lonnie, since you left here for Canada, have been running behind everything wearing a skirt. Lonnie does not even remember to take Trevour to Gravesend Beach for a seabath, even although the place full-up with tourists and hotels and foreigners. Not even on a first Sunday, then, Lonnie come round for Trevour the day after you left, to take Trevour to the Race Pasture. Trevour came back in here nine o'clock in the middle of the night. Nine o'clock. You know that I puts Trevour to bed, every single night, at six o'clock. Nine o'clock in the hands of a police who says that Trevour was loss. Trevour, my only grandchild loss in Barbados? The police say they only guess and by luck, they find out who owns Trevour. Is that the man you sending money-order after money-order to? Lonnie walks about here telling everybody that he have a woman up in Canada supporting him. He tells people that. But I am only your mother, and you don't have to support me. And I am not even going to ask you for a cent. I will not lowrate myself to that, to ask you, who I bringed in this world, to put yourself out and send me one farthing. I brought you in this world. I send you to school. I didn't have the money in those times to send you to high school and Queen's College, so I did the next best thing; I send you to learn needlework at the best dressmaker in the island, Miss Wharton, and you learned with her till you became the best dressmaker in Westbury Village. I turned round and joined you in St. Mary's Church, and you have sang more than one solo, at Easter and Christmas in the choir. And you sang so pretty one Christmas morning, that even the white man from England who used to be the sextant in those days, had to shed a tear in my presence and to my face after the service, and say, "Mother Scantlebury, your daughter may be poor, but she have the voice of an angel." That is the kind of mother I was to you. If I were really a woman of means, if I have the wherewithal, do you think you would be any blasted needleworker today? I would have send you to Queen's College or St. Winifreds, and make sure that today you would be back here in Barbados where you belong, and you would be a high school mistress, or a doctor or a lawyer, anything but being in that cold ungodly place, Canada, working for white people and servanting after people who don't know how to treat you as a human being. For no matter how poor we were you know that we always had a maid to bring you a cup of tea if you wanted one. And I want you to know now, and remember it, that after your father walked through that door, that sad Saturday night, you was only a babe in arms. You must always remember that. And you will understand what a struggle it was to raise you, and I accomplished that, through thick and thin. I am going to warn you this last time. If you don't intend to get a message through some of the decent friends you have down in Westbury Road, that your child, Trevour, spend this coming Christmas in a Almshouse cot, and that I had to spend it in the Poor

House, you hads better get up from off your backside fast, and send down some real cash down here, real soon.

I had to get Freddie the civil service fellow to write this letter to you for me. I didn't post it before now, because I was still waiting to see if just in case the postman was going to ring his bicycle and stop at the house and hand me a letter from you. But seven days pass and I have not heard one word. Freddie was just on his way back from lunch, and I ask him to please finish off the letter, adding these few lines that you are reading now, and post it when he get in the Public Buildings. Freddie turned into a very nice gentleman these days. I wish that Freddie and you had made up your two minds and get married. And Freddie is nodding his head now, in my presence as he writes this. He is is a man of wisdom. A civil servant. But it was through you, and he agrees with me, that you allowed him to get married to Pats who had a child from him three years ago. They are living together now in a lovely stone bungalow in a new subdivision. He is a Brother in the Christian Mission Church. And Enid, child, you should hear him testify on a Sunday night. It would make your heart bleed. Freddie is what I call a perfect gentleman. I do not know why you didn't follow my advice. Today, Freddie would have been my son-in-law. But I am leaving you in the hands of the

Lord. I hope He talks to you. And I hope more perfect state of good health than they leave me, feeling real rotten concerning your child, Trevour, and number two, in regards to Lonnie.

With love and affection,
Your Mother.
(and from Freddie)

It is the 20th o' December, Christmas five short days off, and things ain' improve for poor Enid still bedridden, and the bills and the landlord, the Hydro people, the Telephone people, all o' them bitches riding that poor girl like a racehorse. The pain that was in Enid shoulder blade, whiching as I said had work down all through her left side, well, it now gone back up in the shoulder. Enid found a half o' lime, half-rotting, and she rub it round her forehead to get little relief from the constant headache. Somebody start knocking down the girl place. Is the time when the postman does generally come round. This time, she swear, it got to be the postman with good news, cause nobody can't get bad news every day for a week. Life can't be so rough. Well, it was a strange knocking, and this cause Enid to play she sleeping. Postman don't knock as a rule saving he have a big important letter. The knocking went on and on, and Enid headache feel like if somebody wire her head with electricity. She get vex as hell and throw open the door and shout out, "What the hell you want?" A man standing up there get frighten for Enid voice, and he barely had voice to ask, "Is your name Miss Enid…?" "Yes yes yes! this is her!" And bram! the frighten man drop a blue piece o' paper right in Enid hand, and bound down the stairs, saying, "Thank you, miss, thank you, miss…"

It wasn't no Christmas gift, nor no postcard the man left. It was this:

THE FIRST DIVISION COURT OF
THE COUNTY OF YORK, BETWEEN

High Style Fashions for the Careful Lady – Plaintiff
  and
Miss Enid Scantlebury, 46 Asquith Avenue, Toronto 5,
Ontario – Defendant

CLAIM

The Plaintiff claims from the Defendant the sum of $195.00, being the amount that is owing to the Plaintiff by the Defendant for goods sold and delivered to the Defendant by the Plaintiff, as per statement hereunto annexed.

The Plaintiff further claims the costs of this action and other relief as the nature of the case may require.

DATED at Toronto, this 16th day of December.

B.W. WHITE INCORPORATED

1 Eglinton Avenue East

Agents for the Plaintiff

First Division Court of the County of York

J. F. Wilkinson

Clerk

At this stage, Enid went mad. Everybody out to hang this girl. She rush to the telephone to call Dots, a Barbadian girl who had come up with she on the domestic scheme. Dots' line was busy. She tried to call CROWN TRUST, but that line was busy too. Enid turn black-and-blue with rage. She look for writing paper and she bottle o' *Quink* ink which Lonnie had given her as a going-away present. But she found only the writing paper. She couldn't find the fountain pen although she did use it half hour ago to write the landlord. And then she find it. No ink. So she put the pen nib under the cold water tap and when she went to write she address, the ink was the colour o' cold water. Christ! She start one bad stewpsing, sitting on the bed, getting up from the bed as the headache start up, sitting down again, walking bout the room like if she was a lion in a room. Just then the phone ring and it make she jump. "The Bell people ain't take it off, yet!" she say, vex as hell that the phone ain't disconnect. She vex and she don't know who she vex with, but she prepare for the bastard at the other end.

"Hello, hello, hello?" she shout out.

"Hello?" a voice say, in a nice way.

"Yeah?"

"Is this Missis Scantlebury?"

"That is my name!"

"Well, I'm sorry to bother you, Missis Scantlebury, but…"

"What you calling me? *Mistress*? Look, man, my name is Miss Scantlebury. I am a single lady."

"Beg your pardon, Miss Scantlebury. Your name was referred to us by a young lady, named…"

"Wait! What you telling me? *My* name was refer to you? By who? Who by? Who the arse now been spreading my name all over Toronto, that you, a complete stranger to me, could call me up on my phone and tell me…"

"Missis Scantle… Miss Scantlebury, please, just one minute… we are not trying to sell you anything… All we are asking you is that you permit us to place in your home one of our beautiful sets of Encyclopedia Britannica, as part…"

"What the hell do I want with a Encyclopedia Britannica?"

"Well, we thought that you might like it for reference…"

"Reference? What the hell I got to do with reference, or referring, or refereeing, or whatever the… Look, I don't understand what you telling me, at all."

"… and for study, Miss Scantlebury. We also have for you a gift of the Oxford Concise Dictionary. *Eight thousand* pages, plus an appendix. Or you may choose an Atlas. And, and… Miss Scantlebury… we could make you a present of, ah… are you there, Miss Scantlebury?"

"I still here. Talk!"

"Well, as I was saying Miss Scantlebury, you could make a lovely Christmas gift with the Atlas, for a friend."

"Who give you my name?"

"A lady by the name of Miss Dots Cumber…"

"Look, be-Christ, man!…"

Enid clang down the phone after she call Dots all kinds o' bitch and bad names. She even call the salesman-man by a couple o' bad words, before he put down the phone. Enid dial Dots' number again to tell Dots a thing or two about giving out her number, and when she put the receiver to she ear, the phone was dead. "Them blasted Bell people…" she rattle the phone two more times, but it was really dead.

When the postman did come that morning, Enid didn't know. Passing from the bathroom where she decide to comb her hair and fix up her appearance a little bit, since the pain and the sickness didn't wearing off, she happen to see this letter push under the door:

Haggatt Hall
Bridgetown
Barbados
The West Indies
17 December

Darling Enid,

You have been in my heart, morning noon and night; and sometimes, in the middle of the night also. And at those times, it is because a damn dream has take me up in its hands, roll me all over my bed from side to side, tossing me all over the place, topsy-turvy, and make me think that you are in my bed with me, beside me. And be-damn, when foreday morning does come, I am licked out and smashed up, and panting for you like hell. A wet dream. That is what the absence of you does to me. I am longing like hell for you, in a certain fashion and manner, Enid. I am longing for you. Christmas knocking hard on the door. Rediffusion playing Christmas carols for so. I hope that you still thinking about sending me a little something. Cuthbert say that the three-piece suit going to cost too much dollars for the making, and more dollars for the various taxes he introduce in this island. And he tell me yesterday that if I don't put that forty-four dollars of payment down, including tax, inside his palm first, the suit is not touching my back Christmas morning, at all. I have my eyes on a nice two-tone pair of brown-and-whites, from Fogarty. Your mother — I will have something later to say about her — make me a silk shirt two months pass. She say at the time that the shirt was for my birthday. My birthday come and gone six weeks ago. I have not seen the shirt yet. Seeing as how things are with me and your mother, I will be looking for a next silk shirt. And you know something? I see Freddie the man you used to know before me, and when I see him, he was wearing a shirt that look something like the material I know my shirt is. I am hoping you could see your way and put in extra dollars for the shirt.

I remain,
Always in your Heart,
Lonnie, the man.
Roses are red,
Skies are blue,
My love is true,
Until I dead.

All Enid could do when she read Lonnie letter was to laugh. But it really wasn't no true true laugh, though. It inspire she to write one to the landlord, cause she had something to tell him. Lonnie could wait till she had more strength. Cause she spend all finding the *Quink* ink.

46 Asquith Avenue
Toronto 5,
Ontario
December 21

Dear Mr. Landlord,

I got the letter you sent me. And I get the message too. I am only writing you to explain certain things to you which you don't seem to understand. These is things that happen to coloured people only. So let me tell you some of them. Do you expect me to make blood out of water, or out of stones? Do you expect me to move out of this apartment, when I can't even use a phone this sad morning to call the moving people — if I really and truly did intend to move out. But I do not intend to move. No. You have to learn a few things about coloured people, Mr. Crown Trust. Is that what you say your name is? And it is this. You are dealing with a West Indian, a Barbadian. You are not dealing with one of the stupid Canadians walking about this place. You are dealing with me, Miss Enid Scantlebury, a bred and born Barbadian. And you are not going to frighten me, nor scare me, and come and trample over me just because I happen to owe you one or two dollars and merely because I am far from my home.

I say that only to say this. I have not got the money right now. I do not have it. I am sick in bed. My mother, poor soul, write me last week to say that my child is poorly down in Barbados. I got a letter a day or two from the First Divisional Court people. They claim I owe somebody nearly two hundred dollars. The telephone coming out soon. The Bell people decide on that. The Electricity people, the Hydro, threaten that by December 24, if my bill of one hundred and thirty dollars not paid, I am going to be eating my Christmas dinner in the dark, and opening my presents under a tree without lights if at all I have either of them two things for Christmas. I don't know what the hell to make of my life in this cold country. Everybody here asking me for money, everybody in the world. Enid, we want money. We need money from you, Miss Scantlebury. Enid Scantlebury, you owe we money, we want money. The Lord have mercy, Landlord, what am I going to do? You tell me because you have a damn lot of money, and a damn lot of things to say.

I am,
Your tenant, Miss E. Scantlebury.

PS. The phone just ring with a message for me from Cooksville. The job there already taken. Christmas four days off. Miss E.S.

It looking now as if Enid can't stop writing letter, and dirty letter at that! But she vex with the world. And she find the *Quink* ink, and she have the fountain pen in she hand, so she decide to write one to Dots case she vex with Dots too. Dots the person who give her name to the sales-man-man. She take up four sheets o' paper, the pen full-up with ink, and she sit down, meantime the headache pounding like hell. Strength gone outta she body, and a bad feels take hold of her. So she didn't really try write down the words in the letter to Dots, she only imagine them. But this is what she write to Dots in she mind:

"Lissen to me, Dots! I know you now three years going on four, and you value my friendship so little that you would spread my name…" But she couldn't even imagine the bad letter she had in mind to write to Dots. After all, if she had to leave the apartment, if the landlord really get on like a bastard, then it is only Dots she going have to run to. So she ask God to forgive she for the evil thoughts she had in her mind concerning Dots, and she say, to sheself, aloud, "God forgive me." She did feel better after that. The headache stop pounding, and she really get some relief. She even start thinking about the kind o' apartment she going rent after this sickness. She plan she life from top to bottom, and she make up she mind that if only she could get over this ailment then she going to make a proper woman of sheself. Well, she went to bed, and had a good night's rest. Morning break nice. Enid get up. She wash out she mouth. She pour a little warm water in a glass with Listerine. She laugh, when she remember a television commercial talking about "jungle mouth," and she hold back she head and gargle. The morning start off fresh. Headache gone. The pain working itself outta she system. She sit down over some cornflakes, which is all she had in the house, and she talking to God. Same time, the postman interrupt she, with a letter push under the door.

December 22
c/o Dr. and Mrs. Reuben Rubenstein
Forest Hill Road, Ontario

Listen to me, Enid,

You make that the last time you ever pick up a telephone and call my employer place and discuss my personal business over the phone with her. You understand me? I was shame-shame when the Doctor break the news to me. Canada is already rough enough. I do not need you now to come and muddy up my waters. Allow me to earn the few dollars from these Jewish people. Never, never, never again do you ask Mrs. Rubenstein to lend you money because you and me are friends. Business does not get conducted like that. You are a disgrace to black women who come up here to better themselves in this damn cold country. We who have come up here, struggling. But we also contriving. If we could do it so can you.

God help you, and goodbye.

Mrs. Dorothea Maynard

The only relief Enid had that day was from a thing somebody push under the door, with this written on it:

THE CANADIAN TUBERCULOSIS SOCIETY
Dear Friend, Buy Christmas Seals
Help support your Tuberculosis Society

"What got in me to come up here to live? I would give the world just to be back home now, or be able to talk to a friend, or to have somebody I could call out to to bring me some warm tea and a Phensic or a asprin… God, if you ever bring me through this test, I going get a job, and when I have that passage money, back to Barbados I going! This isn't no wholesome place for a civilize person to live…"

CROWN TRUST COMPANY, INC.
23 December
Miss E. Scantlebury
46 Asquith Avenue
Toronto 5, Ontario

Dear Miss Scantlebury,
We have been patient with you. We think we have been fair with you. You leave us now no alternative. Within the next two days as of this date, our representa-

tive and a bailiff will visit the apartment and remove from the premises your possessions in lieu of settlement of your outstanding rent.

Regretfully yours,
CROWN TRUST COMPANY, INC.

The same day this letter come, one come from Dots. Enid was in such a bad mood that she tear up Dots' letter even before she read it. But when she was picking up the pieces to throw them away, she eyes catch a phrase which wasn't so bad, after all. So she sit down at the table and piece the letter back together again, and when she was doing it, she laugh out, and say, "Looka me though, nuh! I worse than Humpty-Dumpty! Last time I do a thing like this was when I was a little girl and in love with a little boy in the village…" From the pieces she could make out:

… But it served you right, because you are a woman with too much pride. Foolish pride is what I call the kind of pride that you have. If you had only opened your mouth in the proper way… We are one girl. We are one and as such we have to stick together… lesson from these Jewish people who stick together to win battles and victories. I understand now what problems you are having because the Telephone people inform me that they had to take out

your phone temporarily... but that doesn't kill. Be-Christ, we never had phones in Barbados when we were growing up, and it didn't kill us... Enid, honey, forget everything that I said to you in my previous letter, and forgive me. I am going to come down and see you Christmas Eve, and I am going to make sure that I bring you some of my mistress turkey and her husband scotch with me, for you and some mints pudding, and we will stay in your apartment. Happy Christmas, darling, although it hasn't come yet, but we will have a ding-dong time! I sorry that you didn't speak your mind to me instead of to my mistress. But bygones be bygones. And don't forget that the first year when we were new immigrants in this big wealthy country call Canada, we had a nice job and all the eats to eat and drinks to drink, and we were lonely as hell. So keep your tail betwixt thy legs, and wait for me to come down.

Your dear Barbadian friend,
Dots, who...

"Heh-heh-hehhhh!" Enid bawl out, "my God, that Dots is a sweet bitch, in truth! That woman is really a friend, a friend in need! A friend in need is a friend indeed."

Enid was so pleased and happy with the letter that she just put her hand out and take up to phone to call Dots and tell she that she sorry sorry that everything went so wrong. But the phone wouldn't work. This girl's life now turn into a mystery story. Strange and terrible terrible. The phone ring a few minutes ago, and she answer it, and it was a wrong number. "How somebody could call in and I can't call out?" This was a next mystery wrapping up her life in this country. And then... footsteps moving about in front her apartment door... and then they went back downstairs. She move the chair she had put to block up the door so the landlord couldn't break in, in the middle o' the night and catch she napping. She move the chair and she listen. Few minutes later, she hear a scraping noise under the door. When she look and see the thing, she take in a gasp o' breath. A envelope. She snatched it and without reading the address it had on it she slip it under she pillow. She went back to bed trying to catch a sleep, because the headache was pounding again round the temples. She force sheself to sleep, trying to think of Christmas Eve back in Barbados, trying to imagine she was in Barbados, in she mother old board-and-shingle house in Westbury Road, on a day like today, the 24th o' December, Christmas Eve, when *the varnishing and the polishing and the cleaning: the fresh fresh white marl from the rock quarry spread in front of the house in place of snow because there never was any snow in the island and nobody never see a thing like snow fall there even on a Christmas Eve and she mother house smelling like Christmas and the smells*

mixing with the smells of the golden apples of the bananas
of the puddings of the cakes great cakes sponge cakes sweet
bread baked pork and boiled hams and the rich yesterday-
completed material for the new drapes to put at the win-
dows and the window-blinds make in haste by a rattling old
sewing machine that went round the whole village like a
library book and the voices of the late drunken afternoon
singing carols and cursing and laughing and abusing some
neighbours who was too poor or too tight to give a rum or
give enough rum or enough eats or enough money if they
didn't have none o' them Christmas things to eat and the
voices and the laughing and the cursing moving away from
under the early morning window and the rattling old
library book of a sewing machine testing the kindness of a
next black man or black woman who behave as if his name
was Scrooge, and then the tears start to roll down Enid
eyes, and she must have cry for hours for time pass from
she, and memory pass from she, and while she was
sleeping the lights in the apartment went out. Time pass
and when she did open she eyes and jump up thinking
she was in the old iron bedstead with the flat grass-mat-
tress and she pass she hands over she eyes to rub out
some o' the sleep, and then pass she hand over the light
switch, there wasn't no light. She search round in the
dark and find a new bulb. The last one in the apartment.
And still there wasn't no light. A piece o' panic get in
Enid, and she went back sitting on the bed. Time must

have pass, she was thinking. She look through the Judas hole in the door where the only light in the place come from, seeing across the hallway, and she eyes catch Mr. and Mrs. Dick Williams coming home with large parcels in their hand wrap in Christmas paper. Mr. Williams' face was red with the colour o' drinking, and Mrs. Williams' face was blandish and vague and it didn't look real at all although she was wearing mascara and pencil marks for eyebrows and artificial cheeks of red paint and goodwill and Yule and too many martinis which she knew Mrs. Williams uses to drink even when it wasn't Christmas Eve. Mr. Williams and Mrs. Williams stop at their door. Mr. Williams sag a little bit, he get the key in the keyhole, he glance back at Enid apartment door, he say something like, "Merry Christmas, neighbour!" and he then stand to one side while Mrs. Williams walk into the apartment as if she was dancing a waltz and a foxtrot at the same time. Before the door close behind Mr. Williams, Enid see the sparkling stars of light and silver paper on the Scotch pine Christmas tree and she see two overeating pink children jump from somewhere behind the tree and shout out, "Merry Christmas!" when they see the new presents their parents had in their hands. And then Enid see the door close. And then Enid see Father Christmas head hanging from the Williams' apartment door over the doorbell, and Father Christmas head had a real stupid smile on it...

...and time must have pass some more, for a nightmare wrap Enid round its thighs and she thought she had Lonnie in bed with she. But when she realize it was only a dream and she release sheself from the prison of she imagination she was only holding on to a letter which some mysterious hand had push under the door earlier this Christmas Eve evening. She rip open the letter, because there was nothing else she had to do for the whole evening. There was not a blasted thing she had to do, because Dots didn't come down for Christmas, as she promise Enid she would come down. So Enid read the letter:

CROWN TRUST COMPANY, INC.
December 24

To All Our Wonderful Tenants
GREETINGS! Crown Trust Extends the Season's Greetings to Our Customers and Clients. May the New Year Be Even Brighter than the Last. Wishing You All A Very Merry Christmas and A Prosperous New Year.

CROWN TRUST!

...Enid didn't know nothing about time now, and she didn't really know where she was; here or there; but she find sheself ripping the Christmas postcard and the envelope in pieces no bigger than small postage stamps and she fling them in the toilet bowl, and press the flush. Then it must have been a long time afterwards that she sit down on the toilet bowl to pass water, and as she sit there she cry and cry and cry out, "God! Where the bloody-hell Dots is with a little piece o' Christmas cake for me this evenin?. Good God!" When she finish passing water, she get up, and as she flush the toilet bowl she ask God again for a piece o' Christmas cake and for Dots.

On the
Midnight Train

I

He was dressed in baggy pants, in a Harris tweed jacket, and was comfortable with his reflection in the glass, for he looked like a professor: plain, and without fastidious-ness about dress. He wished he had a dashiki to wear. And beads and a silver bracelet and silver rings made from a bent spoon or fork of Oneida silver plate.

He knew his way around this part of the southern campus. It was raining hard. He picked his path through the long grass under cover of the trees, holding his lec-ture notes inside his jacket, pushed into his waistband, to keep them dry. In this thick greenness, with no one behind him, and no one sharing the path, coming towards him, it was quiet, it was peaceful. He felt safe. He felt safe walking under this umbrella of trees, which he saw as there to partially protect him from the pelting rain.

As he emerged from the trees, stepping onto the pavement of the walk, the pavement of the quadrangle, the pavement of the steps down from the quadrangle and into a square garden of cement and more pavement, and some flowers that had been bent and broken by the force of the now-stopped rain, he was still alone as he mounted the thirty-five steps to the auditorium. There was something about steps that he'd never tried to divine the meaning of; he always counted them. Going up, going down.

The auditorium was a poured concrete grey. The walls bore the marks of haste and anger: "Power to the People," written with the spray of many colours. "KKK is a mother." "Black is." "Black is Beau"…aborted. He could never understand why, in this place where most of the people were white, there was not one sign appealing to their dislike of blacks. Perhaps they had been written, and had been erased by the more evangelical hands of the minority. "Black is…"

All of a sudden, it occurred to him that he might be at the wrong building. There was no one in sight. It was the same emptiness he had known in another town, in Toronto, on Sunday afternoons at five, when the entire population was indoors, and he had roamed the immaculately clean streets where no paper blew on the pavement, where no cigarette boxes were left from Saturday night, where he was lonely as a dog trying to find a scrap of diversion on the pavement.

He pushed open the door to the auditorium. Noise exploded around him. It stunned him. The auditorium was packed. All white people. A large poster of thick red cardboard, with black lettering, announced his lecture.

He felt like a prisoner brought into a large court. He was sure he knew no one present. The largest audience he had ever spoken to was a classroom of fifty young men and women.

"Ladies and gentlemen," Willard Snipe, the chairman of the English department, began.

He stood alone wondering what he was going to do. He remembered he had not eaten for the whole day. His stomach churned. He felt it churn because he had just taken his notes from his waistband, had just unbuttoned his wet tweed jacket, it seemed years ago now, when he was relatively unknown but still the guest of honour at a party held only a few yards from this building; and he had looked at the notes to take his mind off the vast crowd of strangers.

"…and our speaker tonight," chairman Snipe said, "who comes to us from Yale University…" There was thunderous applause. "…where in one short year he has established himself as a national authority on Black Literature, will be speaking to us tonight, on the works of the great American poet and playwright, LeRoi Jones…" scattered applause "…specifically, on the play, *Dutchman*…"

Up on stage, at the podium, he realized the first page was blank, except for the regular blue lines printed on the paper. The auditorium was silent. He turned the next page, and saw only smudges on the paper; and he continued turning and saw nothing, up to the eleventh page. Chairman Snipe, beak-nosed and long-jawed, was saying "...he comes to us tonight, before such large numbers as are here assembled to justify the nation's growing interest in, and acknowledgement of the contribution of these people, and I am sure that the professor's lecture will touch upon at least one salient point, which is, at the risk of paraphrasing him, that the history of the relationship of blacks to whites in these United States does not present any evidence that black Americans, as a group, are any more violent than are whites, or less intellectual, or are more violent to whites, than vice versa... as the professor's lecture tonight will prove..."

The applause was as hard and pelting as the rain through which he had just come. The sweatiness under his arms now matched the heavy dampness of his jacket.

Faces were looking up at him, smiles of strange origin, expectant like the hand of a child held out for candy, raised, and he had no notes.

"...as he comes to us from the West Indies."

There was more applause.

Just as he was wishing the room were not so hot, he heard the whirring of the air conditioners come on in the four corners. He loosened his tie. The noise from the conditioners was like the whirring of the engines of the plane he had taken from La Guardia.

These people had come to hear him lecture on *Dutchman*. He had never spoken off-the-cuff in his life. But he was the acknowledged authority on *Dutchman*, he was a full-fledged professor. From Yale. And Yale was looked up to by all other colleges in the nation. He was carrying Yale on his back. He wondered how Yale would feel, if he stood much longer, silent, on this empty platform, behind this wobbly lectern. What would Yale care?

Sirens sounding from outside hushed the audience. They seemed to cock their ears to listen. The sirens grew louder, and then they trailed off; and then there was the humming of the air conditioners. He did not feel any cooler.

"It is important to know," he began, shakily, for another siren seemed to rush close by the auditorium, "it is important to know, that in spite of the tendency toward myth, not even the president of the United States can refute the fact that Lula in *Dutchman*, by confronting the black main character, Clay, is performing an act of violence."

The applause that erupted gave him a scare.

"The act, Lula's act, is conceived publicly, and officially, needless to say, intellectually, more as a matter of correction, of law enforcement, or even as an act of discipline."

He heard applause and other voices, but he was really listening to his own voice. Then he nodded to himself. He said nothing for a few minutes; there was nothing to applaud.

"The attitude has become a national intellectual one, and it is given its strongest emphasis in *Dutchman*, the attitude being that the powerful in their relation to the powerless, have the right to chastise and to correct deviant behaviour."

The voices had become shouts; shouting approval of the points he was trying to make, or not; he couldn't tell the difference, could not distinguish one face from another, did not really know what he was talking about, had not planned it this way; had not planned it at all; but was merely drawing upon all the phrases he had heard and heard again, and had read.

The audience hushed. He did not even hear the voices he thought he had been hearing outside in the town. He saw, for the first time, that he was surrounded by glass, squares and rectangles of glass that had no architectural merit, except that they let in the sky, the dark green trees, shaking and dropping large drops, shaking in more than one direction in the wind.

The audience was not breathing, waiting for the next thing he would say.

Something like lightning streaked the dark greenness in through the large glass wall on his left hand. It flashed once more. And then he looked to see if he could see its origin, and he saw that the lightning was diffused: it was not lightning, it was a fire; but it could not be a fire, since the trees and everything else that was flammable had now been drenched for hours.

"She is a woman with an attitude that is national in its paranoia. She is. She has not offered her apple only to a lifeless character, like Clay; in a Clay-like situation, she has offered it to me…"

There was no breath in the audience.

He felt he had spoken long enough.

"…she held the apple in an act of violence before me, and before Clay. It was also an act of power. And it is this powerful act which determines what behaviour is deviant or consistent with the laws that are established for the maintaining of that sexual power.

"The power of definition is also the power to define."

He could think of nothing more to say. He had come to the end. They did not know it. While he struggled to remember what he had been saying, he stood hoping for some considerate gesture, hoping for some way to hide his shame. His eyes went to the back of the auditorium, and there, to his complete surprise and shock, was a lone black man whose hand, his right hand, was held up at an angle of sixty degrees from the floor. The hand ended in a fist, stern, defiant, acclaiming, proclaiming, comic, bitter, improvisatory and in sharp contrast to the white dashiki and white slacks he was wearing – this black man.

The strong, sinewy black hand glistened under the fluorescent lights; the fist opened and the black man, raised, began clapping in the rhythm of a song by Marvin Gaye, a mocking rhythm, a scornful rhythm.

The audience, discovering that the only black person among them was showing his appreciation through this rhythm, joined in the applause and started to clap their hands, but unwittingly destroyed the rhythm in their enthusiasm because their hands met on a different beat.

There was still something he could see through the wall of glass, something in the sky, burning the greenness of the trees, blowing in the wrong direction for symmetry and for rhythm.

"Right on! Right on!" the black man was crying, "Right on! Right on! Right on! Right on!" above the din of applause.

He wished he had the courage to raise his own right hand in a salute as the burning light, in its sudden brilliance, revealed the huge trunks of the trees, the light rising with such fierceness that he thought it would engulf the campus, and take the building in which he was standing along in its yellow blazing grip.

Before he knew what was happening, Chairman Snipe was beside him, hugging him, the stale smell of cigarette smoke on his jacket and the smell of whiskey on his breath.

"Excellent!" Chairman Snipe said. "Excellent. I hope, as I said in my letter to you, that you will consider seriously being with us, to organize our black studies program. I've talked with Yale and my administrators, and they're agreeable, if we can reach…"

He searched the crowd, now cluttering the exits, for the lone black man, who'd been so conspicuous in this white crowd, but he was gone. The chairman was talking about the offer.

"We've arranged, with some little struggle from the faculty, you'll understand, to give you a tenure track position. Excellent. Excellent. I myself particularly like your conclusion. 'The power of definition is also the power to define.' How many times I've tried to make the same point in my sociology class. But tonight, you've said it better than any social scientist!"

He did not know what the chairman was talking about. He could not remember having made that point. He could not remember saying any of the words, which, obviously, he had to have in order to fill up the hour, the words that had brought such applause, and now, from the mouth of the chairman himself, approval and an offer.

He thought he heard shots from behind the green trees.

"Let's go to your reception," the chairman said, holding his guest's arm, pointing him away from all the people at the back, exhaling his smell of cigarette smoke stale and heavy, and languid as rainwater on damp wool. "The other faculty members're waiting for you…"

He went down the side stairs from the speaker's platform, following beside the chairman. The auditorium was nearly empty. He wondered why, the couple of times that he'd been in this southern town, he was always in the company of only one man. He had never walked beside two men, not at the same time. And he had never had the pleasure of walking beside a woman. Not one woman. Not once, since he had come to this town, "with all these beautiful black broads," as a black taxi driver had said, to which he had added, "pulchritude."

He noticed on his way out of the room, with the pressure of expectancy and the nervousness that preceded the lecture now past, that the auditorium was actually a very large classroom, with desks and chairs arranged in rows, and elevated towards the back, so that when the lone black man had appeared, his black fist had flashed against the whiteness all around.

Chairman Snipe raised his hand, with a cigarette in it, and pointed him toward the reception in the privileged quarters of the faculty club. There was no one in sight. He could not understand where they had all gone;

where they could have disappeared to, so quickly after his lecture. He felt they should have remained outside, on the pavements, as in Barbados, when an audience, done with the lecture, spilled onto the pavement and tore the lecture apart, and put it together again, with their better wisdom.

The light he had been seeing beyond the trees had sunk, and was now merely the remnant of the sun.

"Such a beautiful sunset," Chairman Snipe said. "With these long days, and with so much rain, it's a privilege to stand here as a free man and watch our sun set."

II

Why was he so lonely, adrift, unanchored and unhappy? If he looked around him, in the broadloomed room of Persian rugs, table lamps and books in so many places, on tables, on the floor, in chairs, that he hardly had space for his large scotch and soda, why did he feel so much the stranger among these men and the few women who smiled at him each time they crossed to the bar, each time he lit his pipe? Why did he feel it was so difficult for him to accept their kindness, their smiles, their snatches of congratulation? "Fine speech," "Fine lecture," "You really taught me something about this country" and: "I never looked at things just that way. You provided me with a new way of seeing old things!"

Why was he so intent on regarding himself as un-
suited to this well-heeled, well-fed, hard-drinking crowd
of professors and their wives; and why was he now certain
that he had once before been in the company of that
black-fisted man in one of the back streets that bordered
the black area of town, sitting in the doorway of a country café, *checking out the sounds, what's going down*, as the
man had called it, listening to Marvin Gaye and Aretha,
Sam and Dave and John Coltrane, a music as strange to
him as rock and roll and bluegrass country guitars; forced
to snap his fingers and nod his head to the loud beat, "like
you ready to lay down some moves, man." Why could he
not relax, crystal glass in hand, with three ice cubes at
swim in whiskey, as he nodded to expressions of approval?
Why could he not put back his head, plump against the
soft pillowing of the wing-backed chair? Why had he not
felt free to say in that country café that he preferred
Beethoven's *Fifth Symphony* and his *Third* to Marvin
Gaye's "Get It On Up," that he was more at ease with anything by Mozart, than he was with Aretha? Not that he
disliked Aretha. After all, it was she who had accompa-
nied him on his first performance of cunnilingus; and
there was something, after all, like the eating of fresh
fruit, to be said about that activity. Peaches. That's it, he
thought, sitting in a Queen Anne chair as if he owned it,
it was the taste of fresh peaches: biting the teeth into it,
and having his lips touch the filament of skin.

Slouching, he continued trying to take his mind off his discomfiture in these academic surroundings, polished with wealth and good taste in furnishings, so, instead, he studied Chairman Snipe's long-jawed face weather-beaten by the crossings of time, an element of travel in the face; arrival and departure; his body bulky, pudgy, as are the fingers of both hands. On the right, and beside it, on the little finger, a wedding ring, a family heirloom, an emblem or crest of some sort. He is amazed that he is able to absorb himself in such small things. Chairman Snipe has the girth of a man who likes to eat, who likes to drink. A happy figure. He wears baggy black trousers, black socks, dark brown sandals of a determined German make and design. When he takes off his jacket, he is in a short-sleeved blue shirt, with a tie.

As a small boy, dispatched four times on a Sunday to church, to matins, communion Sunday school and evensong, he wore a short snap-on tie.

Chairman Snipe's tie is not a snap-on. It falls over his imposing belly. His belly is, without doubt, the focus of all his emotions. He wears it proudly. He does not try to button his jacket. He does not try to draw in his paunch. He does not try to pull his trousers over it. It cannot be covered. He is not ashamed of it.

Studying Chairman Snipe's belly, he was sure that he again heard shots being fired in the distance. But in the drawing room, on the edge of the Queen Anne chair, he was far removed from shots and guns being fired. No one was hearing the jazz being played – as if no one wanted to hear the riffs of the alto saxophone and the piano chordings, but wanted only to have a musical distraction behind the determined conversations about black studies and "the place of *Dutchman* in the spectrum of American belles-lettres."

"On what basis," a professor was saying. "On what intellectual basis can we include a work like *Dutchman* in a credit course of English Literature? On what grounds? The point I am trying to make is, that even if we considered it as part of our course in Modern American Literature, there still would not be the intellectual basis to justify its inclusion."

Again he thought he heard the *ping ping* of bullets.

"In South Africa," the professor continued, apparently tired of his own argument about black literature, "in South Africa and in Northern Rhodesia, to give two well-known examples…"

"But why don't you bring your argument and transplant it to the United States?" another said.

"Are we any better here than South Africa or Northern Rhodesia?"

"In this double standard, we live the way we do, because it is mainly in the United States that there is…"

"Has always been."

"The point I was trying to make…"

"I'm sorry."

"…is that there has always been considerable social intercourse."

"We are not graduate students here! Make the point. In other words, confess. Considerable *sexual intercourse*."

The chairman was speaking, patting the tail-point of his tie against his stomach.

"There has always been considerable social *and* sexual intercourse between whites and blacks."

"You mean blacks and whites."

"Why the differentiation?"

"Doesn't he know?"

Again, Chairman Snipe was speaking.

"The most important thing about a book I've been reading in manuscript, is its title. *White Over Black*. White *over* black. It could not have been different – black over white – without a different book having to be written."

Nine men, five women, himself, four forty-ounce bottles of Dewars, three bottles of Jack Daniels, one bottle of rum from Cuba, one bottle of Gordon's Gin, one bottle of vodka. He could not pronounce the Russian name on its label. All half empty.

The voices in the room were rising.

"The schizophrenia of this country, whose antecedents have maintained a double standard…"

"And of which the country itself has become suddenly and painfully aware, according to the latest issue of *Esquire*…"

"The double standard is now being questioned by the heightened social awareness of black Americans."

"It is being questioned also by the white American, just as seriously, for it is this white man whose misfortune it is to witness a black successor and heir."

"We can always bless the black American with this problem."

"Bless him, or blast him."

"*Newsweek* carried an excellent piece. On Martin or Malcolm."

"If the law had punished improper social intercourse and sexual intercourse, between blacks and other nonwhites…"

"Are we in South Africa?"

"Apartheid, you mean?"

"Well, now that you've mentioned it! The point is, ontologically speaking of course!"

"That is no point."

"The fact remains that this apartheid would, filtered through other American myths, crystallize the illegality of such intercourse."

"We *are* in South Africa."

"The time has got to come, as we gathered from our colleague from Yale…"

"Yale, our mother university! Is that what you're hinting?"

"As our colleague from Yale, soon to be numbered amongst us, said earlier tonight, at the moment that the white American can afford to believe that the primary inhabitants of the *Dutchman* are..."

"Which is, euphemistically, blacks."

"Blacks."

"Well, say blacks."

"Okay. Blacks are not non-people, then..."

"Then, and only then, to overstate the case, then and finally, will it be possible in this country to be sane, and at the same time presume that the inhabitants of *Dutchman*..."

"Blacks."

"Blacks."

He heard the shots again, outside the drawing room. But no one flinched, no one went to the window.

"By the way..."

It was Chairman Snipe.

The four forty-ounce bottles of Dewars, three bottles of Jack Daniels, the bottle of rum from Cuba – was it Cuba, or Jamaica? – the bottle of Gordon's Gin and the bottle of vodka, whose name he had already given up trying to pronounce, were all down to a quarter full.

"By the way," Chairman Snipe said. "Did you notice the fellow at the back? Do you know him?"

"You mean the black!" a professor said. "With the black power salute! Did you see him?"

"If I were you, being a stranger in these parts, particularly…"

"What the good doctor is trying to say is, as a West Indian intellectual, your fight is not *their* fight. Have I synopsized your sentiments, chairman?"

Chairman Snipe ignored the assistance.

"Do you know the fellow who gave the salute? What I mean to say is, I hope you don't plan to…"

"Birds of a feather, chairman. Birds of a fucking feather!" another professor said.

Chairman Snipe scowled, knitting tight his thick eyebrows.

"You have a future on this campus. I would hate to think that you might jeopardize it, being a West Indian, by that kind of… a precipitous association. We want you down here. We want you to consider the offer, seriously, tenure track isn't often offered in the South," the chairman said.

He read the label on the large Dewars bottle; he tumbled more whiskey into his heavy crystal glass. He overpoured. He spilled a lot of whiskey on his jacket sleeve. He saw the chairman's overhanging tie, placid upon his belly. He could hardly hear Dave Brubeck and Paul Desmond playing "Time Out." Something was happening to his eyes.

He should go. He decided to go. One o'clock in the morning. Time, someone said. Chairman Snipe placed his hand, which was soft and puffy, on his damp tweed jacket, on his shoulder, with no force, with no weight of emotion in the touch, with no indication that the gesture was hale, as in two fellows well met.

"Yes, it's a short walk, but maybe it's best you take a taxi. No? No taxi! Okay. Safe home y'all. Safe home."

III

In this darkness, in this strange land of more rain than sun, he shortened his steps, unsteady, as if he were, being a little drunk, about to stumble. He was on a street bordered by wide green lawns. Even in the darkness, he could see that the houses were painted white. All the houses he had seen, during the daytime in this place, were painted white. There were no lights in the houses. Some were almost hidden by trees. He walked in the middle of the road. The road was straight. He shuffled forward, sidewinding from curb to curb. He could smell patchouli, old water and mud. He smelled of whiskey. His sleeve was still wet, from elbow to cuff. He felt the weight of his bladder. He knew he would have to stop in front of one of these large, tree-hidden houses to pee on the lawn. He knew he had taken the wrong way, as he edged up onto a lawn, his right shoe toeing against something soft, about to unzip his trousers. He stood still above the rising stench of dog shit. The grass was wet; the sweet smell of fresh-cut grass cleared his nostrils as he wiped his toe, while noticing a moving light around the corner. He moved, and the light moved, too. He returned to the middle of the road, shuffling on.

He stopped under a signpost. The name of the street was Hyacinth Circle. To his left, he saw three tall, shiny white columns holding up a white-painted house. He thought of Rome. He thought of Greece, he thought of all the textbooks he had studied back in Barbados; he knew he was in front of the courthouse.

That afternoon, the local newspaper had carried a front-page story about three black men who had been sentenced to ninety-nine years in that courthouse.

"Ninety-nine?"

"Ninety-motherfucking-years, plus *nine,* brother!" he'd been told by the college's dormitory porter.

The courthouse square was wide and sprawling with many benches, but he figured old white men sat on those benches in the afternoon, chewing tobacco and expectorating the dark brown tobacco blood. Beside the old white men would be some black men grown old early, with felt hats that had sweat stains round the hat-bands, bright-coloured braces, checkered shirts and shapeless trousers. They would be smoking cigars, their faces creased in painful, suspicious intensity.

"That the motherfucking courthouse," he said aloud.

Hyacinth Circle thinned into a lane; the canopy of trees had a smell, but he had not learned its name. The smell that still travelled with him was that of whiskey. He had a sleeveful of whiskey. He did not think he had drunk so much.

There was a light at the foot of a driveway. Not bright. It was mounted on the left pillar. As he got near, he saw that the pillar was wooden. The pillar turned into a post; nothing like the Roman or Grecian pillars he had seen farther back. The number on the post was 432. He knew a house somewhere, a house he had entered often, with the same street number. He wondered where he had seen that house last. He walked up to the post. He loosened his tie.

By the light on the gatepost he saw a clump of grass, thick and strong, and he could see its roots. He remembered back in Barbados, in his father's "ground," pulling pond-grass from choking the potato-slips and the young yams. "To pull-up this kind o' pon'-grass, yuh does have to grab-on pon the clump by the root, at the bottom, then, and ease-she-out." His father had said that.

He squatted down, grabbed the plant by the bottom, wrapping his fingers round the root; the dull light from the gatepost hitting him in the face, just as, years before, in another place, he had bent down, with the sun hitting him full in the face.

He got the clump of grass: devil-grass, pond-grass, or blue-grass, as they called it in this part of the world. He wiped the root over his sleeve and the lower left side of his jacket; he smelled now more of the dank earth than of slovenly drunk.

He moved off.

Under a canopy of trees over the road, he was walking now in almost total darkness, down a slight incline. He felt the strain and the muscles in his legs register and balance the other muscles in his body. A sign said North Jefferson Street.

He looked back, and there was nothing; nothing, except the sound of the night, which was like the breathing of a woman who has asthma.

The incline became steep. He could feel the muscles in his calves. Two dull lights seemed to follow him, shone over his head and pointed to the trees thinning out.

His jacket felt heavy. His shoes were hurting his corns. He remembered a story he had been told about corns and bunions and black women.

"Why not black men, also, have bunions?"

"Because the black woman walks to work, on her two feet; stands up and works, on her two feet; is fucked over from behind by the master, while on her two feet; and at the end of a sixteen-hour day, she turns around, and walks back, on the same goddamn two feet, in the same goddamn shoes! She deserves to have her corns *and* bunions."

George Washington Street North and George Washington Street South met North Jefferson Street. There were suddenly no trees. The intersection was like a parking lot, with wooden houses, lights still on in them, only a few yards back from the curb, with no grass on the lawns in front of the houses. He could no longer smell patchouli and wet grass.

Under a weak street lamp, he searched in his jacket pockets, then his trousers pockets, and finally his shirt pockets. He had no money. He had no wallet. He had no passport, no Blue Cross card and none of the five identifying pieces of Yale plastic he'd been given.

George Washington Street, North and South, was a highway. The white lines were clear and painted thick, on the black asphalt. He looked right, he looked left. In both directions, there was only darkness, tight, a rustling in the darkness all round him, and the asthmatic sound of the wind.

He saw some men and women far down the highway. He could see them rocking from side to side, walking in the distance as if they had no feet, like sailing boats in an accommodating sea, with a slight but assisting wind.

He knew where he was. He had been in the country often enough to know, to associate Jefferson, Washington and Wilberforce on street signs with the areas where only black people lived, even in crowded, large cities.

The road was wide. The men and women were closer. He was passing high brick walls on both sides of the road. He realized he was walking between grave-yards; large thick crosses were embossed in the brick; bottles or vases, shimmering in the night, with sprigs, flowers, dried leaves sprouting from them. Of a sudden, the road was bathed in a bright light from powerful over-head lamps. He could see names on the plaques in the walls: *Benjamin Washington, died 1899*. A former slave? Certainly black. His name betrayed him. *Julius Jefferson Walker, born 1898, died 1950*. Then he saw a name that rooted him to the earth. Perhaps he was dreaming. He read the name a second time. The date of birth. The date of death. He became frightened. It was *his* name. With the correct spelling. And with his middle name, too.

He threw aside his jacket and rolled up his trousers and made a jump at the wall, but it was too high and too slippery with moss. He made another leap. There were no cracks in the well-made, sturdy masonry of the wall, to put a hand in, the toe of his shoe. He took off his shoes. His third attempt was hapless, he was too tired.

A slowly moving car pulled up behind him, its dull lights had become high beam headlights. They showed him a gate. He ran to it.

As he stood inside the gate of the graveyard, the car with high beams came abreast. He felt chilly though the night was hot and humid. He started to panic. He could see the face behind the car window. And he could see the shield on the ten-gallon khaki-coloured hat, the roll of fat on the man's belly. He could see the gun that lay against that belly. He tingled with sweat, fear, excitement.

The car had *City Taxi* written on the side.

He had been told, most taxi drivers at night are cops.

He had never seen a state trooper before. The trooper was eyeballing him.

"You work here, boy?"

He didn't understand the fat drawl to the vowels. But he caught the "boy."

He nodded.

"Burying many, today, been many deaths lately, boy?"

He nodded.

"Two o'clock is a goddamn early hour to start, ain't it, boy? The early bird getting on them worms. And this here is a ripe enough worm farm. "

Without a word of goodbye or good morning, the cop moved on, easing the car forward, off the shoulder by the gate, on to the highway. This was a dream, he thought. It could have been, it should have been a dream.

The graveyard was not well tended. Clumps of grass grew between graves and in the paths. A beer bottle held a sprig of a flower, now dead and withered. A cheap vase held a cluster of flowers; one white bud was still alive. Some graves withstood a towering architecture of tombs; little houses with no windows, and no doors to let in a breath of redemption or allow the escape of a doomed soul. Some were merely mounds, like fat bellies upon the body of the earth, wet with dew. Among all these, he did not find a cross that bore his name. But he had *seen* his name. It had not been a dream, not as close to unreal as the state trooper in his taxi, with his belly and his gun.

He was far from the iron gate, down a knoll, and into a small gully, still thinking about the state trooper's strange behaviour. Why hadn't he gotten out of the taxi – if it was a taxi – to order him about, to push him, to slam him against the peeling paint of the car door, to spread his legs like wishbones, to pass stubby fingers over his groin, touch his testicles, feel up his buttocks, perhaps weigh the heft of his scrotum in the palm of his hand, to cuff his wrists with iron bracelets, to dump him into the backseat of the cruiser-taxi cab…?

Overhead the trees were large and healthy, a rich emerald green. They were not fruit-bearing trees. In Barbados, where there was a graveyard on a beach, where English sailors had been dumped after they had been shot at sea, there were small, brown, gnarled trees that bore fruit. Beach grapes. He had eaten the fruits of those sailors' graves. In this graveyard, there were no trees he knew by name. Where the outside walls met at a corner, at right angles, where it was very dark, and there was a smell of fallen leaves rotting, he hunched into a squat, his trousers down to his ankles, but clear of the rotting leaves, arms crossed, his spine arched, muscles in his back tightened, head bent down, eyes flashing right and left, in case of real grave-diggers who come to work early in the morning.

"Cleanliness is next to godliness."

His mother had often said this to discipline him. Here he was, going to take a shit.

The moment he closed his eyes, there was a loosening, a relaxation of the bowels, and he surrendered his body to indifference, an indifference at being caught.

With his eyes closed, and in the easing of a simple function, the thing that came out of him, slipped to a sliding end and was on its own cut off there in silence on that space of land.

IV

The lone black man who had given the power salute to the crowd at an angle of 60 degrees, an audience of academics, all of them white, came at him out of the high noon sunlight, crying. "Bro, call me Calvin, you and me, we going to lay down some saving shit this night."

He had said he was a doctoral student, when he called him at the dormitory.

They agreed to meet, Calvin promising to pick him up in his "aut-o-mobile."

It was Saturday, late afternoon, six o'clock, the skies cleansed so well he could have been in Barbados. There was a constant breeze like a sea breeze though they were inland, a tinge of coolness to the air.

Dressed in a black dashiki, sleeves and hem trimmed in red and green, Calvin sat alertly behind the steering wheel of a small Volkswagen, holding himself erect.

"Didn't tell you I had me these wheels, eh brother? Thought I would be driving me some big wheel deals from Detroit, didn't you? Well, shit, I says to myself," and he put the car into gear, so they could drive off. "I says, shit, let me make a protest and be radical with a foreign car. Boycott the Detroit motherfuckers! You dig? Got me these Nazi wheels off a none-too-bright white student. Two bills. Two of the lean green. So, here we be, you and me. After what you *been* through, shit, I thought you could do with a bit o' sightseeing. Paperbag's in the glove compartment, sippin' whiskey, bro. Just keep the bag *down*, if you see a cop.

"An' I don't know," he said, slowing down, "if you can handle this shit, brother. You West Indians are some crazy bastards. Where we are is where you were walking that night. What you thought were houses, only they is garages or servants' quarters, Jack. Matter o' fact, you ain't seen nothing! There be houses, *estates*, that would make your motherfucking head *turn*.

"Dig that place over there. With the white gatepost, with the light? That light always be burning. Day and night. Rain or shine. Sonofabitch living there got more bread than Paul Getty. The mother got some mean-faced dogs trained to kill black people only. No postman delivers on foot. Mother's got a special car, Jack! Aut-o-mo-bile! Special delivery.

"All these estates along here, all along Hyacinth they got private guards, private dogs, burglar 'larms and *guns*, so any crazy motherfucker wanting to integrate the massa's property, he be looking down a double-barrel. I know. Almost got my ass tore up, bro, by two Kraut dogs.

"Shit! And here I is. I be driving German wheels, and the rich be keeping German bloodhounds! Ain't that a bitch? Integration. We and them be radical protesters against the American system."

"Can a dog be trained to attack only blacks?" concerned that he might sound naïve.

"Only blacks?"

"Isn't a dog colour-blind? Like a child?"

"Ever read *White Dog*?"

"Not yet."

"Check it out, brother. Blacks? Niggers! Tear up their ass! Check it out, before you start strutting your stuff through a neighbourhood like this, especially after six o'clock."

"Six?"

"Six be the hour to leave town, brother. You broke curfew that night. Cowboys and crooks. Western Justice. Rednecks and rascals. That house back there, with the gate lights? That's the *man*. That's the Klan. Nineteen miles due south, man, the Klan was born, so, being a social scientist, you can figure out how many of those mothers along Hyacinth still have their cards and their sheets. But they don't come out even for the full moon, these days. We got their names, we sent 'em postcards, man. Neighbour Dan is the man in the Klan, Jack!"

The VW, rollicking and wobbling along the road, passed the pillars he had seen in the night, except they turned out to be the white-painted posts of a gazebo holding a swing and white-painted iron chairs and tables. The grass was precision cut, in the brush-cut hairstyles of the American Armed Forces. And the grass was blue. More blue than green. There were men with mowers and men, bent almost like hairpins, who stood close to the grass, as if they were examining it; and from his safe distance in the VW, these men looked like large wild mushrooms because of their wide-brimmed hats worn against the sun, and probably, too, against recognition. They moved their hands, like mechanical toys, as if playing with the grass. Showers of grass trimmings rose up on the wind. These men looked as if they were growing out of the lawns, natural to the habitat. Even when the land, in this present dispensation, belonged to other men.

"If you can kill any one of those mothers cutting the grass, or any black for that matter, with one shot in the heart, *three* in the back of the head, and then have a sheriff say it's an act of justifiable homicide, and have white liberal intellectuals write books and end up agreeing, then according to the logic they taught me in Logic and Scientific Method, 105, certainly a man like me, a nationalist, should be able to kill one of them mothers and demand that what I do be called an act of justifiable homicide. Dig it?"

"Calvin, you got that out of a book. Not your ideas. Not even your words, never mind your thoughts."

"I was writing a paper."

"This thing, this thing that's going on in this country, which is your country, has really got screwed up. None of us can even talk in a natural way. We can't even fire a pee, by the side of the road, without analyzing our piss, and calling it an act of defiance. I pee on a wall of a house owned by a rich white man, and I am therefore making a Marxist statement."

"But you *shat* on the man's property, Jack! *Shat* mister-soon-to-be tenured man."

"Graveyard communal property."

"You kidding? The gate light house? The man that owns that estate, he owns the land the graveyard is sitting on."

"Justifiable homicide?"

"For goddamn sure! And dig it, agree or don't agree, I say your act was defiance. Was revolutionary, brother. How many niggers in this place would *dare* to shit on a burial ground? When I gave the story out to the brothers, they agreed you was a real mother. Matter o' fact, those brothers'll be at the club tonight. Waiting to meet the new *man*. Drinks, and not Ripple shit this time. *J & B! J & B!* And ribs!"

"I don't usually shit in cemeteries. It was an urge of nature."

"Urge, my black ass, brother! You ever had the urge to hump a white chick you meet in a shopping plaza? You ever had the urge to tell a professor, Fuck off! You ever had the urge to grab all the bills in a bank? You ever had the urge to rip off textbooks, because you had no bread? One day, you will join the motherfucking struggle. It's blood, brother. It ancestry. I don't give a sweet goddamn how much West Indians like to own houses and save money in the bank, and get their goddamn education, it's still *blood*. You were *safe*. You motherfuckers from the islands be even more crazy revolutionaries than we with all our Panther shit when the man tickle you in your ass. Check out Marcus Garvey. You West Indians be field-niggers more than house-niggers, as Malcolm X says.

"But dig, I checking out a book last night, blew my goddamn mind. I was reading this thing, I start to think. What the fuck am I getting this *ofey* college education for? Why the fuck am I not in the ghetto, close to the brothers, checking out the scene. The *real* scene. Making it real, man, compared to what? Building a nation, a black nation, what the fuck I'm writing papers on Black Aesthetics for? One minute, my model is Ralph Bunche. Then he's a Tom. Then it's Martin. But Martin get his ass whupped, on television, in the newspaper, and I was there at Selma. So, I want to have Miles, or Coltrane be my idol. Man, to blow all night. Let the sounds that go round do it. Like Barry White says, Let the music play. Let the motherfucking music *play*, Jack.

"I'm Miles. Coltrane. Otis. I'm Nina. And I'm *Areefub*! On stage. Thousands be out there, in the darkness, heads raised up, in wonder, Jack. My voice. My trumpet. My axe, man. Same fucking thing! Same fucking instrument. Let the motherfucking music *play*.

"So, I'm checking out this book. A slave narrative. I been blowing my brains out writing papers on philosophy, white philosophy *and* black philosophy, and the philosophy of philosophy. I been breaking my bad ass on

Black Aesthetics and juking my way through Judeo-Christian ethics. I been in graduate school for the past eight years, book by book, index card by index card, Xerox by Xerox, borrowing, stealing and inventing notes to make sure, brother, that not another mother in my graduate seminar can match belly-up to my grades. And for what? What goddamn for?"

Calvin slouched in the driver's seat.

"After all that shit, after eight years of cops with guns, guns, and billy clubs, Jack, an' after I'm fucked up with revolutionary rhetoric like a motherfucker in my brain, I come across a goddamn slave narrative."

"A slave…?"

"Check this out."

He brought the VW to a shuddering stop. Under a tree. In the shade. He moved his body in the driver's seat as if he were improvising a shuffle. He ripped open the brown paperbag that held the Ripple, and placed the bag on his head, like a hat, and chanted:

"Howsomedever, one day Mars Walker – he was the oberseahfoun; out Dave could read. Mars Walker wa'n't nuffin but a po' bockrah, en folks said he couldn' read ner write hisse'f, en co'se he didn' lack ter see a nigger w'at knowed mo' d'n he did; so he went en tole Mars Dugal; Mars Dugal sont fer Dave, en ax' 'im bout it.

Dave didn't hardly knowed w'at ter do; but he couldn' tell no lie, so he 'fessed he could read de Bible a little by spellin' out de words. Mars Dugal look mighty solemn.

Dis yer is a serious matter,'sezee; it's 'g'in de law ter l'arn niggers how ter read, er 'low them ter hab books. But w'at yer l'arn out'n dat Bible, Dave?'

Dave wa'n't no fool, ef he wuz a nigger, en sezzee:

Marster, I l'arns dat it's a sin fer ter steal, er ter lie, er fer ter want w'at doan b'long ter yer; en I l'arns fer ter love de Lawd en ter 'bey my marster.

Mars Dugal sorter smile en laf' ter hisse'f, like he 'uz mightily tickle bout sump'n, en sezzee:

Doan 'pear ter me lack readin' de Bible done yer much harm, Dave. Dat's w'at I wants all my niggers fer ter know. Yer keep right on readin', en tell de yuther han's w'at yer be'n tellin' me. How would ter lack fer ter preach ter de niggers on Sunday?"

He could hear cars roaring by; in the distance, he heard the heavy rumbling of a freight train. Even in his small home country, in his small chattel house, he had heard the sagas of freight trains, men on the run travelling on them. Men in chains rode on them. A rumbling that was interminable as a toothache that came at sunset in a dark small room when the only light was the dull golden snuff of a kerosene lamp. He heard a siren. An ambulance?

He heard Calvin's unscrewing of the bottle of Ripple.

"What you make of that, Professor?"

"Fucked up. By our education."

"What education you talking bout? Some few sociology books written down by people who don't know dick, and don't like us?"

"The man in the story, *he* understood the importance of education…"

"The Bible, it was not invented for you and me, brother!"

"We can use it to suit ourselves."

"You're talking like my grandmother."

"My grandmother said the same thing."

"They were fucked up, too, then, brother."

"They survived. They survived."

Calvin lit a menthol cigarette. After Calvin had filled his lungs, and had shot two thin jets of white from his nostrils, making him look in his moment of anger like a walrus, he said, "We are over-educated. And our education still excludes us, you and me, you a professor and me, a goddamn graduate student, from all the intellectual considerations of this country. So, what can we do?"

"Revolution?"

"We got to express our own conclusions, man, black conclusions, our own fears, black fears and feats, our own black aspirations about this country, in a different language."

"You mean a different rhetoric."

"Yeah!" Calvin said, as if he wanted to have said that himself. "Yeah! A different motherfucking rhetoric. An antagonistic rhetoric, too!"

Through the tinted glass of the VW, he saw concrete, and scraps of newspaper, and paper wrappings blowing along the sidewalks. There were trees but no flowers. He longed for the softness of light and the colours of New Haven. He wondered if he was not irresponsible, longing so much for the North. The South he had always been told was the place where he *belonged*. "Why don't you goddamn go down where you all come from?" But he wanted the softness of red brick, dirty red brick, the tidiness of streets shaded by small trees, he wanted the gently aged appearance of old houses, their dereliction untouched by rioting. Here, the sidewalks, the streets, were too exposingly bright. He wondered if any serious thought or honest intellectual pursuit could ever be achieved under the scrutiny of such brightness. Such instant delineation. Perhaps, people here, in this place, had to wait for the night before they could be comfortable, before they could see into their minds with meaningful clarity. He knew that the deepest, reddest blood was shed in such concealing nights, but still, maybe the nighttime was the right time to be black. He felt entirely confused, his vision clouded by smoke from the mentholated Salems and the vibration of a passing freight train.

Calvin had been deep in his own thoughts, but he must have come to a conclusion, or some agreeable compromise with himself, for he straightened his spine; his eyes were bright, and the whiteness in them shone. His dashiki took on a nobility, despite his cut-off blue jeans.

"I'll say this last heavy shit, brother. I'll lay this heavy shit on you, and then, I promise, we'll enjoy ourselves for the rest of the day."

He was a man who, to make a serious statement, had to light another Salem. "There's obvious dangers in generalizations like this. I'm talking bout the sickness in my country, the sickness that is the obscenity going round this country, even among young radicals like me. I'm talking bout the feelings of ambivalence that eat my guts sometimes. Still, America is my country. And America is one vast, no matter what shit going down, one motherfuckin' mass of landspace, time, and ideas. And in that vastness, in that bigness, for we Americans like bigness better than quality, in that bigness and vastness there's gotta be a proper diversity of ideas. For, believe it or not, brother, certain judgments gotta be made. If only for the motherfucking purpose of convenience."

"Jesus Christ!"

"That be the word, brother-man," Calvin said. "Judgments gotta be made, some serious shit of convenience and inconvenience has got to go down. Now, let's get down, afterwhile-chile."

V

It was a long white road. Calvin slapped a tape into the tape-player. "My Favorite Things," that tantalizing hymn to a new harmonics on the tenor saxophone, a solo that gave him the same feeling as going to church in Barbados. The sun had just gone down behind the tall casuarina trees. There was a slice of a moon, at dusk, thick green sugar cane fields on both sides; and he was walking in the middle, far from each edge of the field, his black shoes shined with the puritan's love of labour, for Sunday, were covered with the white dust he kicked up, with his hurried, frightened step. The church bells, chiming with hope for the repentance of sins, were as repetitious as the trees, lined and planted stiff on a parade square. Each time John Coltrane repeated his main statement, he heard the monotony of the tolling bells, charming him out of his waywardness. A charmed pull, this same bending of the neck toward the small speaker in the VW, brought back to him the chording of the bells, and beside him was his grandmother, content, for she had travelled many times before this path of anticipated Pentecostal salvation. In the same way, beside him, Calvin drove silent: for he had heard all the places and things and colours which the music had showed him before. The tape had been played many times: "My Favorite Things."

In the distance, was a barn? A factory? Something like a semi-portable camp for soldiers? It sat stubbornly, squarely, without any architectural grace. It was black from this distance. It was a club.

The tenor saxophone reminded him, by harping on variations of the same theme with precision, of the singing of old women, his grandmother, leading the service-of-song in the Mothers' Union meeting, repeating "Rock of Ages, cleft for me, let me hide myself in Thee…"

A neon sign told him he was approaching the Eagle Club, a black building, the siding being made of black, tarred shingles.

And the neon sign did not tell the truth. The first letter, "B," had burned out.

It was the Beagle Club.

Calvin parked the VW at the end of a line of cars. He sat very still listening as Coltrane played "A Love Supreme."

A love supreme, a love supreme, a love supreme… Nineteen times.

He got out of the VW. Because he was wearing a loose-fitting, pocketless dashiki he had not brought his pipe; he had not brought his tobacco pouch; he had not brought his English leather – *genuine leather* – gentleman's wallet; he'd had no room for his fountain pen with black *Quink* ink, and he was not travelling with his address book. And, he realized he had made a mistake about his comparisons: it was not the old ladies and "Rock of Ages, Cleft for Me." It was himself, chorister in the chancel of St. Michael's Anglican Cathedral, singing a song of praise. Easter? Christmas? Rogation Days? Quinquagesima Sunday? Lent?

> O, *all ye beasts of the sea*
> *Praise ye the Lord.*
> O, *all ye fish of the sea,*
> *Praise ye the Lord…*

That was it! That was the comparison. That was the repeat, replete with the beauty of the saxophone.

"Some heavy shit's going down in here, brother-man."

"*Cool.*"

Calvin looked at him. "Every time I git down with Trane playing 'A Love Supreme,' I gotta smoke me some weed, and…"

The main door opened, there were tears in Calvin's eyes. He was not crying. He was happy.

"Can you handle this shit, brother?"

He said no.

"This shit'll kill you. It's a motherfucker."

"Cool," he said.

"'Love Supreme' is a motherfucker. Freaks me out. Least five times a day. I have a joint, shee-it!" He took a deep, silent pull on the joint that was no longer than his fingernail. "'Love Supreme' remind me of a thing my grandmother used to hum round the house, something white folks call a canticle. Shee-it, more like cuticle to me! But anyhow, this canticle has got itself a Latin name: *Benedicite omnia opera*. Shit, been hearing my grandmother singing it, often is often does:

> *O all ye Works of the Lord, bless ye*
> *the Lord: praise him, and magnify him forever.*
> *O ye Nights and Days, bless ye the Lord:*
> *Praise him, and magnify him forever.*
> *bless ye the Lord: praise him, and magnify*
> *him forever...*

"Check it out, man."

"You Anglican?"

"Baptist bred in the bone! All rib-sandwiches and fried chicken."

The room was dark. Bodies moving. Laughter loud and sweet and black and jocular. Smoke rising and swirling; and it hovered above the lighter darkness of bodies. Like broad-brimmed halos. Music climbing the walls. Live music as he had never heard before. Loud and full, the enunciation of each voice, of each instrument, of each riff, pleading with thick sensual contrition:

Didn't I do it, baby? Didn't I? Didn't I do it, baby?

Towards the front of the large crowded shuffle-footed room he saw Aretha. There in the warm Southern night! He was overcome. He could feel his body relax. He could smell fried chicken. Fried ribs. Tingling burnt hair. Processed hair. Cosmetics and lotions. He could smell and feel his own sweat.

Didn't I do it, baby? Didn't I?...

The large room was like a country of men and women all of the same colour. This was the first time that he had ever entered a space inhabited only by black people. It was a beautiful sensation. He thought of powerfulness. He could feel his blood.

Two women, heavy in the thighs, heavy in arms, heavy of flat broad feet, were together, heavy breasts pressed against heavy breasts, defying a man to force himself between the veins of these two women, grinding out their joy, grinding black coffee hip to hip, a black world they had created through dance, a black world that dance itself had formed and drawn a circle around.

Three rows from the stage, he stopped. He had to. Bodies were not moving. They were allowing no space for his wooden shuffle. He was the only one not in an embrace. Not hip-snapping slowly.

Didn't I do it, baby?

He could see her black face bathed in perspiration, like the water of baptism. He came face to face with the woman.

"Shit, there's more than Aretha…"

He turned his head; it was impossible to turn his body. At his ear, Calvin was smiling round a rib-sandwich.

"There's more singers in the South who whip Aretha's ass…"

"But I thought no other woman could sing like Aretha!"

"For *every* Aretha that whitey make a star, we could up an' provide *ten*."

"They say she's the best…?"

"The *best*-known, but she ain't the best! Not down here!"

"This is somethin' else?"

"What you say?" Calvin shouted.

"Somethin' else!"

"Cool as the breeze… on Lake Louise…"

"This chick be a motherfucker!"

Calvin laughed so loudly that dancers glared at him.

The two women who had been dancing together were now at arm's length, two fat hands holding two fat arms, giving the sloe-eye to him over each other's shoulders; smiling and content. He was relaxed in a world of sound; safe and almost serene.

A midnight train to Georgia...

There were dark lonely roads; there were tall trees; there was the smell of magnolia, a smell he had been told about, but never could identify, so that even now that he was in the South, where the smell was born, he did not know which trees gave it off. There was also the smell of burning flesh, of rotting flesh, of flesh manhandled; but also, always the smell of love. He was prepared to travel all those dark miles of never-ending rails of steel, going from place to unknown place, to remove himself even farther from his present...

A midnight train to Georgia...

He was now in the arms of one of the fat ladies, deep and comfortable against the billows of her stomach, her arms round his smaller body in an embrace so much like his mother's that he felt he could fall off into a sweet slumber, except that the song was raging through the magnolia woods of this land that held such frightening mysteries to him. She held him close, tight. She held her left arm round his waist, and her right on the softness of his bottom. And he, in against her flesh, was moved slowly, very slowly by her, by her body, by her blood, the iron of which he thought he could taste, and so gave himself up completely to the music.

He was not passive in his enjoyment, though his pleasure was so complete in its rapture that he felt as a child. He was as aggressive in the almost motionless dance as she was. Her left hand was grabbing the right half of his bottom; and his hands were pressed deeply into her soft flesh, not entirely out of sensuality, but also because she was so much bigger than he that he had to latch on to her, to apply the imperceptible pressure to move her to the music in his own slow, sweet time.

And he thought of poetry … *green and golden I was huntsman and herdsman…*

"You sticking me?" she said. A breath of Jack Daniels as she spoke.

His right leg was hugging her left leg, the inner thigh. He could feel her weight. He wondered what it would be like if, by accident, or even not so much by accident, she were to fall, full on top of him.

"Is that how you feel?" she whispered into his ear.

And nightly under the southern stars as I rode to sleep, the owls were bearing the farm away.

He searched in his mind for a poem written by a black American, a Southerner, to clothe his joy in, and render his blessings more appropriate. What would she say? What would Calvin say, if he were to know that he was crystallizing this "black aesthetic in white rhetoric?" That he had used a white Welsh poet of wide renowan to capture a black Southern experience? Calvin would say that since the experience was love, or lust, or sex, or the desire for a foop, "It's a universal motherfucker, brother."

"You sticking me."

Her mouth was at his ear. He smelled perfume and cosmetics and treatment, a hot iron, process in her hair. She tightened her grip on him, and forced his smaller body *into* hers and gave a sigh; apparently not satisfied with the press of his body against hers, she tightened more. His breathing became more difficult, and then she groaned, in a sweet, short, spasm. *My wishes raced through the house high hay and nothing I cared... that time allows.*

"You like me, don't you? I know." *The train was entering Georgia.* "West Indian men adores American women."

Wherever Georgia was, or is, whatever the ruggedness of the landscape, whether of rocks or stones, green fields of sugar cane or of cotton, the concluding journey was clear before him. The singer, now bathed in her sweat, sequins moving as she breathed, rippling upwards from her ankles to her arms, her hips swaying, shunting on the beat, shutning like the pistons on the train pulling into town, long after midnight. *Oh as I was young and easy in the mercy of his means, time held me green and dying though I sang in my chains like the sea.*

"You do want me, don't you?"

He could feel it. He could feel the deeper softness of her thighs. He could feel grits in his mouth, tasteless sugar, coarse flour-dust. He was hard. The singer was coming home: the two sequined pistons could now be seen in their slowing-down, and as they dropped at her sides, like a victory that concludes bodily exhaustion, he felt the sudden semen thunder down. And at that moment, in the slowed-down, soft sighing voice of the woman, it lighted upon him.

Immediately, the most powerful fluorescent lights, long and shaded by pieces of aluminum foil, came on, and the room became an arena. The woman held him close, although the dance was over. The strength in his trousers was limber. Across the bright floor, Calvin was holding the hand of the other woman, coming towards him, with schemes written on his perspiring black face. The woman continued to hold him close. He did not want to be released from her embrace. The room was too bright. Too accusing, too sentencing, too condemning.

He looked down to see his trousers, but trying not to appear as if he was inspecting any wet damage to his white Levi's. On the floor, in the harsh fluorescent light, he saw a lady's earring and a dead fly.

"Blasted fly!" he said.

He knew she would look down. And when she did so, he crushed the fly flat into the dust and cigarette butts. And he took the opportunity, rising from the superfluous murder of the fly, to glance at himself. He was safe. He was still hard.

Small boys in Barbados, he remembered, had put their hands in their pockets, to pacify the evidence. But he could not get his hands into his pockets. His Levi's were too tight.

"You like sticking me, don't you, small-island man?" the woman said, and pulled him towards her, embracing him affectionately, overbearing in her fondness for him, as her girlfriend approached with Calvin.

"Fuck it!"

She unclipped a long purse, red as her lipstick, with patterns of silver on it, and from its silver lips, she pulled out a cigarette.

Her hands were broad, thick, her fingers pudgy, short. She wore no rings. She covered his hands with hers.

When she moved her arms, her colour took on the sheen of brown alabaster. He wondered if she was *mixed*. When he turned to catch her words better and looked into her face, he saw that she was a most beautiful woman. Her nose was large. Her lips were full and soft. She wore her hair swept back off her large forehead. "So you's this black brain from up at Yale!" Eyes, big and round, suggested a personality that, while being soft, demure, feminine, also took no shit, not from *anybody*. "Fuck it! We got black brains down here, boy!" She squeezed his hands. "One's standing across from you!"

He looked into the deep, cavernous, black sweetness between her enormous breasts; an aggressiveness, a violence surged in his body. He wanted to conquer this woman.

"Don't mess with this sister!" Calvin warned him.

"Pour this young man some drink," she said. A waiter had just come by. "Give the man a *drink*."

"Can you handle it, brother?" Calvin said.

"With such big brains?" she said. "I heard he got all them white professors on the campus frighten for him. Thass good. We show them."

"Leave my man be. He got to *integrate*."

"Fuck it! Give the man some Jackdanills."

He was given a plastic cup, a black, red and green striped plastic cup. The waiter poured him four fingers of bourbon.

"Can you handle it, brother?"

"Hope you told those *colleagues* o' yours the *truth*," she said. "Hope you told them about Malcolm. Most o' we down here, in the South, favour Martin Luther King. But not me. The church has its place. A place for sitting-in and laying-in, and getting your head whupped. That shit don't appeal to me. I'm as Baptist as King. But my first love is Malcolm. The NAACP's more suitable to the North. Don't ask me what I mean, and how I know. There's enough white liberals up north, and black ones, too, to finance the NAACP. But we down here in the South? We's the field-niggers of the movement. You don't think so, Professor?"

She laid the weight of her hand on his thigh.

"Right on," he said.

"Fuck! This island nigger's jiving like *us*!" she said.

She cuddled closer; and he smelled scent; he smelled hair treatment, he smelled her breath, fresh and clean and with a wisp of tobacco on it. She placed a firm wettish kiss on his lips.

"This nigger's *mine*!" she said with a fierceness that frightened him, even though she laughed as she said so.

Her size; her blackness, her sex and sensuality; her hands; her breasts; and her magnitude. The magnitude of her: that's the word he had been searching for all night to describe her. Her magnitude frightened him, made him feel he was a small man. It was the smell of womanness about her; the funky, sexy smell which put a withering on his hardness. She had claimed him as flesh, as property.

The band started to play, the floor became crowded, and feeling that he was safer on the dance floor, he took her strong hand and led her to the circle of the dance.

The music was very slow. He was hearing Barry White's "I Don't Know Where Love Has Gone." He knew that all he had to do was *lean*; lean on her. *Belly rub, grind some coffee*. Her greater size would do the rest, he was going to relax, against her *fine brown frame*.

But something happened. Out from the saxophones, trumpets, bass guitars and drums came a turbulence that

needed the expertness of lithe Southern black movement. It was *the funky chicken*. He heard a man scream
in glee, "The funky chicken, man!" He was left standing
lost in a sea of bodies breaking their limbs at parts where
there were no joints, doing a soul sashay, a choreography
of spin steps, a barnyard cakewalk, women with their wig
hats and high heel sneakers on…

He was wooden. Like a piece of stick. He could only
watch.

The woman was not interested in his clumsiness, did
not care for his inadequacy. It didn't matter what he
thought of himself; that he was a professor at an Ivy
League college; that he had recently given a brilliant lecture on *Dutchman*; that white men with degrees behind
their names wanted, by tracking him through tenure, to
validate his authority; it did not matter. He was adrift, a
leech, a virus, something that took all the juices of joy
and creativity out of the situation he had entered into,
and he was incapable, not just through lack of talent,
lack of training and lack of exposure, to feel in his bones
now that he was in this midst of this total blackness, he
was anything other than – a transient.

He could only envy, and then hate the bodies of these
men and women bent in ecstasy.

"*Move!*"

It was Calvin, transformed. Though not really transformed. He had always been *that*.

"*Move*, motherfucker!"

Calvin looked like a tall, black pullet.

A chicken, his face blank, flat, and pallid. Calvin laying an egg. Calvin fluttering his wings. Calvin, cock of the roost. With a deep almost imperceptible joy. Crowing; a stubbornness and nobleness; watching for another cock who might challenge him, all this was in the dance.

"*Move*, brother," Calvin said, pleading with him, as one would plead with a man to force him to take the first step to coerce arthritis in the legs. *Step on out, man. Strut your stuff. Keep the jive alive.* Calvin was urging him to reach for the warrior-dancer who dwelled inside, like oil in the land, untapped. "Come on, brother. Ain't no difference between the funky chicken and you standing still doing the belly-rub. *Git on board, professor man. Move it.*"

OUR LADY
OF THE HOURS

When the snow fell like this, when it was night, she was lost in the whiteness. "Why I still in this blasted country? This blasted snow! Me coming home to all this." She looked at the houses along the street. No light came from the windows, not from her two-storey rooming house. "Now, back home, we make one house different from all the others. Bring out the personality of the house *and* the dwellers therein. Lord, look at this blasted thing!" thinking, as she descended into a darkened stairwell to the basement rooms, that she must get out soon of her underground living, this confining hole; she did not know at that moment if she was walking on wooden steps, so deep was the snow; and she stopped a moment under the eave, which was not a well-built eave, for it kept out nothing, neither snow nor rain, and she made up her mind: "First thing in the new year. First thing come the new year, I moving from this blasted basement. Basements're where animals should live." Yes, she would look for a better place, "And I have to put that man who thief my child, absconded with my child, and Lord, I don't mean to be mean and anti-motherhood and anti-my-offspring, but with your strength and guidance, I sure as hell am going to have *soon*, to put that child and father outta my blasted life, *and* get on with my own life. And I *know* you won't hold that against me!"

Thinking of this made her tense and feel unholy, and even though she had sought to cleanse herself of the bad taste of this neglect, this abandoning of her child, she became nervous; nervous as she sometimes felt opening a door and knowing that inside she was going to see that a cat had mistaken her bed all day during her absence, when she was making a living for herself and earning money to buy vittles for the bastard cat, that the cat had shat on her bedspread. This kind of nervousness gripped her, and happily she reminded herself that she did not possess a cat. She had some difficulty getting the key into the hole. She could not see the key and she could not see the hole. Everything was white. Even under the eave, repaired four times for the year, by the landlord. She felt and guessed at the opening.

The smell of the rooms, closed up all day, came at her with a rush of blood to the head. But it was a welcome scent of life. Not like the extreme smell cleanliness gave her when she entered the mansion where she worked in the ravine. And she it was who had cleaned the mansion so thoroughly. And she it was who had made it smell clean; as if people who used the rooms did not live there. But she most decidedly lived here. Incense, which she burned before she left for work, placing it in the soft dirt in the green plastic pot of her favourite dieffenbachias, and left burning like a spirit in her absence, the incense she burned the moment she returned, to help kill the lingering smells of her cooking, especially when she cooked curry chicken and split peas and rice to share with her best friend, Gertrude, the incense filled her nostrils. And there were other smells: the detergents and the sprays that changed the smell of cooking into the faint fragrance of heather. And of course, the scents from the green bottles on the top of the water tank of the toilet, left with their mouths agape, their grey wicks like unhealthy tongues. And of Limacol she used to rub her arms and legs, up high between her thighs, when she felt a strong tension of anxiety or a touch of the flu coming on. And that of her perfume, which sometimes she left open, in her rush to be punctual, to be early enough to stop and chat with the jeweller and with Gertrude. It was the smell of close acquaintance with a room, with a chair, with the floor which was not level and which was covered in linoleum, over which she had placed scatter rugs thrown out by her employer mansion in the ravine.

The first thing she did after lighting two long sticks of incense she always bought from a black man dressed like an African in white robes and a white skull cap, and who called her "Sister" and to whom she said, without a smile, "I am old enough, you hear, to be your blasted mother, boy!" was to stand and inhale the rising wriggling smell of the line of smoke, and sneeze loudly and violently; and then she took the photograph of her child from her handbag. She placed it on the tall unpainted walnut dresser in the bedroom.

Her bedroom was cluttered. It was curtained off from the rest of the large room, the living area, by a screen made of vinyl. Before going to sleep, she always closed this concertina screen shut until it reached the latches which she locked, making certain her body was safe and could not be seen in the squeezed-off small congested room. "Too many oddballs roaming these days, and a woman like me, to be raped..." She leaned the photograph against a bottle of Limacol, which was one of several bottles and vials of pills for headache, for blood pressure, and for the small woman's problem she suffered from, from time to time. Back in the living area, she sat on the sagging couch. The couch was placed against the wall that was shared with the neighbour people on her left side, as she came through the door, the east side, "that blasted side," people who turned up their stereo full blast, and plagued her with reggae, "that heathen music" they played and played and which pounded away at her with its unrelenting beat and drove her mind into a vexatious numbness. But she never complained to them. "A Christian-minded person wouldn't." She never knocked on the wall with a broomstick handle. Never refused to say, "Good morning, my dear," when she met them in the mornings, early and stiffened against the cold and saw them badly dressed for winter, or bright and blazing in colours during the summer, as if they were going to carnival, being Guyanese.

Beside the couch, covered with a printed cloth down to the floor, a cloth of frayed edges, like tassels, was a table covered by the same printed cloth. The cloth had a design of roses. Red roses. She loved roses. That's how it had happened in her landlord's back garden. She had been attending to his roses and talking to them as any decent gardener would when the neighbours, not knowing roses or gardeners or decent people, told the police that there was a mad woman in the backyard talking, going mad over the bed of red roses. That call to the police had required all her Christian forbearance and tolerance to forgive them. After the police had left, she had come in and gone to bed for two days of lying in the dark with her eyes closed. Fully dressed, fully clothed, watched over in the dark by her photographs on her table, framed photographs of her child, in various stages of his growth and development; and also a Bible; a vase with more red roses, this time artificial; a book, *Women*, which Gertrude had given her as a birthday gift last year; a small panda which she had bought for her child, two years ago. And a large teddy bear which Gertrude had also given her, this time for Christmas, last Christmas.

She slept with the teddy bear between her legs, to give her warmth and to keep her company.

She opened the Bible.

She knew which chapter, which verse, which book, she wanted to read. After the incense, and the photograph, the Bible was the first thing she turned to when she returned home from work. Even after a rousing three-hour service, stormy as a revival each Sunday at her church, every Sunday at two o'clock, she turned to her Bible, and sometimes, too, after the midweek prayer meetings and Bible study. She knew the words of grace, the words of repentance, the words required and printed in blood and in gold in the Bible and which words of absolution for herself she would choose.

She opened the heavy, dog-eared book at Hebrews, Chapter One. She passed her little finger down the right-hand of the page, a pointer for her eyes, over the first verse, over the second verse, mumbling the words in speed to herself, but audibly. When she passed her pointing finger over the third verse, it was what she wanted. She began to read aloud. And she said, "God wants to hear a sinner's voice." She had said the same thing aloud one Sunday in church, when the woman beside her had touched her sleeve, an admonishing touch, because she had been reading aloud, following the Collect as it had been read by the pastor. "God wants to hear a sinner's voice."

… when he had himself purged our sins… Yes, Lord!
… sat down on the right hand of the Majesty on high!…
Praise his name!… *being made so much better than the
angels, as he hath by inheritance obtained a more excellent
name than they.* Your precious Word. Yes, Lord!… *For
unto which of the angels said he at any time, Thou art my
son, this day have I begotten thee?…* Yes, Lord! I am thy
humble daughter… *This day have I begotten thee?…*
Lord, if only your Word had said *forgiven*, instead of
begotten! But it is your Word, and I have to accept it. She
shook her head from side to side.

"Hebrews, Chapter One, Verses Three, Four and part
o' Five," she said, as if she were in church, as if she were
the pastor informing the congregation of the passage of
Scripture to be read. "Hebrews," she repeated. "Now, I
am going on my two knees before thee, to ask forgiveness
for today, and what I do and did not do today. Our Father
who art in heaven, hallowed be thy name, Thy kingdom
come…"

It was time for the telephone.

"And how you this evening?"

Gertrude was on the other end. She would put the
world right tonight, as she did every night; and discuss
work, employers, life, as it was passed by in the street,
the jeweller, a conversation which lasted very often for
two or three hours when they were happy and swimming
in the sweetness of gossip, a conversation that would be

about themselves: woman to woman. Tonight, her voice was high and happy; her spirits had been refreshed by her prostration before God.

"I just got up off my two knees, just brush them off, as a matter o' fact to get the dust and grains from biting into my flesh, after saying my prayers, dear. Well, my dear, some thoughts passed through my head today, on account o' that man I works for, that I had to prostrate myself before my Maker and ask why I becoming so evil and sinful in this blasted city."

It was seven-thirty. Gertrude would be in her small kitchen, cooking peas from a can, mashing the Irish potatoes which she liked, and which she ate every day, and frying the steak which she also liked, round steak, which she cooked with a little salt and less pepper, and a bottle of imported beer, Lowenbrau. And before bed, a crystal glass of brandy, Hennessy. Gertrude, unlike herself, had no guilt about not saying her prayers before "she hit the sack." But it was only seven-thirty , and the night was still young enough for their long conversation.

"Why you don't let me make you some curry with some hot peppers and put some vim in you, eh? What about tomorrow night? I notice the last time you eat a mountain, and you didn't complain, and still you saying to me you can't use hot thing? Girl, you always eat my food with a hearty appetite. If we were closer, living closer, I could warm up the pot right now. But mentioning it now, as I crossed this door a few minutes ago, the snow, eh? And I haven't even taken off my coat. I notice just a little smell of curry in this place, and before you could snap your fingers, I had to light some incense, yes, and it must have been that that crossed my mind to make me ask you if you would really like some tomorrow. Yes, I make it hot, to put some vim and vigor in you, girl."

She smiled as she listened to Gertrude's protestations about making the curry, if it's not a problem, if it's not imposing, if you making it for yourself, well, in that case. And not too hot, just right, cause it sets my mouth on fire.

She unbuttoned the three buttons on her winter coat. She loosened the blue warm scarf round her neck. She pulled at the deep blue woolen blouse, and the thick polyester brown slacks, making herself comfortable. A tam-o-shanter of emerald green, homemade and knitted with an amateur knitter's touch, with a large round ball of blue wool in the middle of the skull, was still on her head.

"Mr. Iacabucci, poor fellow, eh? That poor man is still on my mind. Something I was listening to on the radio, down in the ravine house, say it happened the Sunday when the wife was at the hot stove. I think I heard the voice in the radio say that there was three bullets fired at that poor man. The first one missed. And hit the 'luminium lid clean off the pot o' rice-and-peas. Those strong, fat red beans we cook in our rice-and-peas. That thing bout the 'luminium lid off the saucepan o' food is the first ounce o' truth I heard, from all the things that came over the radio and the television. Something worrying me for the last few weeks concerning that man I work for? I am not sure he isn't one o' we, yuh! Anyhow. He is so often times under the weather. I would say that the police is guilty of attempts at 'sassination. Plain and simple. I had cooked some of that rice-and-peas with the Jamaican kidney beans for you once, didn't I? Yes, man. We were watching a hockey game that Friday night! Were you at your television when they were asking for more bigger guns to protect the police from criminals like Mr. Iacabucci? Criminals who threaten their life with a garden fork, muh dear. I bet you, when the truth does come out. And it may take ten years before the truth comes out. The truth concerning people like me. I am not talking about the regular, everyday truth regarding people like you and me, I meaning the *real truth* like the words of the Bible, I would lay my bottom dollar on it. When the pure truth comes out, in ten years, I bet you they confess and admit that Mr. Iacabucci only had a lil spade, made outta tinning, in his blasted hand before those two police go gunning at him. Now, they asking to bear more bigger guns to bore more bigger holes in innocent people."

She remained silent, angry in her silence, agitated as her friend answered her, in words that came from afar, strange even in the way they sounded. She remained silent, listening to the voice she had known for so many years, telling her she was wrong, that the police are there to "protect you and me" – and it made her sad to know that this voice, and these words, were coming from perhaps the only person, woman or man, in this city, in this country, in the whole world, for she had given up Barbados, whom she ever trusted. And still, there was this wide gulf in the way they saw ordinary things.

"It is pure and simple, a case of ordinary sinfulness, Gerts!"

"No, darling. It is merely law and order. And we must have that. Imagine what it would be, if there was no law and order!"

"Gerts, I'm going to tell you something now. And don't get me wrong. But Gerts, if I didn't know you, I would wonder if you wasn't a blasted racist, like the rest of them."

She could hear heavy breathing coming through to her ears. She could feel the hot breath of the breathing. She could see Gerts' eyes, gone smaller, like slits, and see how her face had become red. Gerts' face always went red when she was overjoyed, when her favourite hockey team scored a goal; or, when she was embarrassed by a dirty joke; or, when she had an orgasm. She had confessed all these things.

She ignored Gerts' breathing silence and looked at the face of her child framed on the walnut dresser, the child who had been dragged across the border to America by his father. She was longing for him. She took off her winter boots, using one foot against the heel; and then the other.

"May I ask you a personal question?"

"About Mr. Iacabucci again? Or about me being a racist?"

"About neither."

"Have you decided on the ladies' watch at the jeweller's, at Vladimir?"

"That thief? Vladimir smiling with me every morning as God send, and trying at the same time to rob me. I compare the prices down at Eaton's, Eaton's selling the same ladies watch cheaper, and Eaton's don't know me, and Vladimir smiling with me every morning."

"What, then?"

"I want to ask if you know anything about mental breakdowns?"

"Who's having one?"

"Are there signs you can see, if you know those signs and how to look for those signs?"

"You have to be trained to know. There are books. Lots of books in the store. Lots of things could be signs."

"Is falling asleep one?"

"You and I would be in that state, darling."

"I mean, every evening, recuperating as he is, with a bottle in his hand? And sleeping in his clothes? As Mr. Iacabucci does do."

"It could be. And then again, it doesn't have to be, if you see what I mean. It does not have to be. People like that, they should be helped."

"Can I tell you something?" Her room was hot, her skin hot, her upper arms and legs. It must have been the heavy woolen coat.

"About my racial attitudes?"

"This evening, just before I left. He was sitting in his library, his den. And I went in. To see if there was anything I could do before I leave. If anything was wrong, before I leave. Not that I was thinking anything was wrong. I went in to see something, for myself. And there he was, sleeping, like a little child."

She rubbed the inside of her knee.

"He looked to me so much like a little boy. And there I was, standing up over him… Such strangeness came into my head."

"You think of comforting him?"

"I was shame shame shame at the things that came into my head."

"Like comforting him?"

"Gerts, what the hell do you mean, by comforting him? A woman my age? He is not a child that I should comfort him! Pat him? Run my hand through his head of hair? What the hell you suggesting, Gerts?"

She was laughing into the phone so Gerts could hear her laughing, quiet-like, a suggestive laugh more suggestive than she had intended as she passed her hand up and down her leg. "God! these legs got an itch like all get out in the winter! No, I am not now speaking to you, Gerts!" She was beginning to feel warmer.

"Are you there?" Gerts asked.

She raised her dress above her knees, following the tingling that travelled like a contagion. She looked down into the lusciousness of her legs.

"Still strong for my age."

"Are you speaking to me?" Gerts asked.

She rested the telephone on her shoulder near her neck and leaned her head on it, so that it became fixed in that crook. Both her hands were now free. She could hear Gerts' breathing through the receiver. She turned her dress hem backwards, folding it into a roll, until it reached almost up to her waist. She could see her tight black mound of hair. She placed her right hand there. And closed her eyes immediately. She did not want to see. She did not want her eyes to witness this sin. And it was as if the secrecy and the privacy of the act being committed in her basement apartment, alone as she was, was so sinful in her belief, and for her Christian life, so enormous and so startling, that she could not bear to witness it, could not bear to see her own act, herself. But the sensation was there. Like a sting. Through the receiver, there was a faint sound, as if her friend Gerts had put her own receiver down to perhaps eat another chocolate cookie. There was only a faintly perceived breathing. Perhaps, it was her own breathing she was hearing coming back to her.

"Can I ask? Ask you something? Private?"

The breathing, the silence, the caressing had become one: outside the single window of the basement apartment, heavy wet flakes of white were falling. She was aware of their falling. She remembered airing pillowcases in the backyard, near the white-limbed trees behind the mansion in the ravine, and seeing feathers fall to be carried away in the wind. And she remembered hearing the howling of the wind through the branches of the white-limbed trees. Birches? Those with white limbs! With bird bark. And next door, now, someone turned on a stereo, and the booming of heavy music, steel and voice, tore through the thin wall, her back resting on this wall, leaning against the wall, to be more comfortable; to be relaxed; to be free; to be more accommodating to the demand of her body.

As the music poured through the wall slow, full and thick, the wind piled snow against the glass; and her hand was moving against herself and the sight of the fall of snow silently banking against the window was the only soft relief she had from the pounding of the music next door.

"May I ask you a personal question, Gerts? When you undress at nights, whenever, do you find yourself... How do you undress for bed?"

Gerts said something which she didn't hear.

"Gerts, talk."

"Strip and flop. Strip and flop, particularly after ten hours in the store with books."

"Being alone, Gerts. Being alone, all the time, there's things I do, things I do, like taking off all my clothes with the lights out, even though there's not a living soul here, but me, and these beasts next door playing all this tuk-music which I sure you can hear, deafening me all hours o' the night. Sometimes, I swear that if I don't cover myself in the darkness, one o' them might be at a hole in the wall, spying on me and seeing all my business. Just like their music drives me up the wall. Gerts? Do you know I never undress with the lights on? And I'm in this place all by my lonesome. There're certain things, girl, that I won't dare do, even when I am alone."

She heard a dog scratching at the outer door of the basement apartment.

"That dog again!"

"What?"

"That blasted dog and those sinners next door!"

"You got to kill that dog," Gerts cried. "I tell you that before, so many blasted times."

"Oh God, no, Gerts! My God! I can't do *that*. Poison a dog? No, man, that isn't Christian. I couldn't do that. How would it look to see my name in the papers, and on television, arrested and charged and in front of a judge… oh God, no, Gerts!… and some o' them judges as racist as the police!… and out in prison with a lot of blasted women, wickers all o' them, and you can never tell what dirtiness women do in prison, what would happen in those circumstances? If I was to put some ground-up glass bottle on a bone and feed it to that blasted dog, I don't wonder what would happen. Perhaps, where you reside, a person can do that. But up here at Finch and Steeles, where there's all this crime and people unemploy, and undecentness, and rapes every other day, they would swear there's a connection between the colour of my skin and such action. Not me, darling. That blasted dog again!"

She moved away from the thin wall through which the music was vibrating against her body. "Anyhow, you ever undress, and stand up naked in front of your bureau, or look in your bedroom looking glass, in that state? You *do*?" She burst into a laugh, aware it sounded a little forced. "And do you inspect your bubbies, your breasts, in case of cancer? You do that every night? And don't get a certain sensation when you doing that? No? But do you inspect other parts, though? Even with the lights out? Not me, girl, I still feel a little ashamed to be looking at myself in that way.

"Gerts, I never thought there would be two women in this world, two women who are so different in certain ways, with different jobs and education and schooling living in two different places and we could be going through night after night, the same womanly tribulations o' life! Image that, eh? And you give yourself an inspection in the bathtub, too? I have a teddy bear. And child, I enjoy, I *just enjoys* playing with that thing as if it was a child, and I was the age of my own child. Blasted dog!

"But let me ask you this now, Gertrude. Do you think that these feminine things that we do, and have to do, being women living alone, are things we really should not be doing, because they are the actions of a child? And I never broach this to you in all this time, but in all this time whilst talking to you, I find myself touching myself, a thing that was farthest from my mind and intention. And I have seen loneliness that you could cut a knife with. And if you don't mind me telling you this, Gerts, cause the truth is the truth. And honesty is honesty. But I really enjoy doing it. I really and truly enjoy myself. Even though it is sinfulness. According to the Bible. It started out so innocent. You know when you come in from outside in the cold, into a house that warm, and the cold outside this week is so damn terrible, that you feeling as if your very bones is turning to ice? The sudden change in the temperature? And in your body? It started out as an innocent thing, like a sensation…"

The dog was still scratching against the metal frame of the storm door.

"… can't understand, and I never will understand certain people. I am talking bout these brute-beasts living next door to me. The music. The loud music. The loud music all hours o' the night. And now the dog. The dog all hours o' the night. And if I tell you, Gerts, that they are social workers. Blasted social workers. You won't believe that people who make such a critical fuss over people on welfare, can you explain to me how they could allow another living creature, namely their dog, to be out in the cold on a night like this? Is minus-twenty? I mean, even me and you. Grown women. In our two homes. And we still have to seek…"

She made a face, a tense face, pursed her lips, and began shaking her head.

"… *sisterhood*? Is that the new word? I hope it doesn't mean nothing else! Like wicking! Well, sisterhood, then. Although I never heard such a word. I must look it up in the books that Mr. Iacabucci in the ravine has in his library shelves. But as I was telling you, those two damn brutes who call themselves social workers don't really know the first thing bout God. Or the meaning of niceness. Or humanness. To leave a living creature out in a night like this? What you say the temperature now?"

"Freezing."

"Below?"

"Minus."

"Minus hommuch, my dear?"

"Twenty to twenty-two."

"Lord have His mercy! Not even a dog, no, not out there in snow so deep. Let me call you back, Gerts."

She went to the front door. The dog yelped, squeezing through the crack of open door that also brought in a gust of wind and cold, a cold that drilled an icicle of pain into her shins. The dog danced in frantic circles on the linoleum.

She closed the door, slotted the three bolts, and locked out the cold and the night.

"Let me feed this dog some milk," she said.

The dog sprawled on the linoleum, whopping of its tail on the floor.

She opened her small, white fridge: there were wedges of cheese in yellow plastic wrapping; bottles of soda water "for gas"; tomatoes and apples wrapped in cellophane; milk in cartons, one carton of homogenized, one of two per cent; pieces of ginger bought months ago and looking now like deformed fingers; tins of marmalade and jams from Jamaica; plastic containers of rice, peas, rice-and-peas, roast beef, roast lamb, roast pork; and bottles of tomato paste, bottles of grapefruit juice, five containers of yogurt, for losing weight. "I gotta get rid of this food. Tummuch food for one person!" and, top shelf, front and centre, her bottle of Hennessy Brandy.

A two-burner stove stood beside the fridge; two saucepans of split peas and rice, and a stew of braising beef, pig tail, carrots, onions and mushrooms. When she lifted the lid, the dog drooled. But she gave it milk. In a white Pyrex bowl.

"Not my stew, you brute-beast!" she told the dog, who was lapping up milk noisily. "I muss walk through tummuch cold to bring this food, from down in the ravine, to this place, for me to waste it on you. You a blasted stray dog!"

She ran her hands over the wet fur of the dog, and then poured Hennessy into the crystal brandy snifter. She was thinking about the Commandment concerning strong drink, knowing that the Hennessy was more than "for medicinal purposes, Lord"; and all the time she sipped, she knew the dog's eyes were on her, she could feel eyes spying on her from behind the wall; next door eyes, eyes she was sure watched her undressing every night, the eyes of the blasted ghost of Satan upon her. She poured a double shot of Hennessy, Satan's ghost the strong justification of her indulgence.

She began to undress for bed. She examined her legs and thighs, and her breasts; and she stood in front of the looking glass on the bureau, and tried to see her whole back, from the neck to her lower spine. The dog was bent into a hairpin, biting into its wet fur. She wished she had double joints, was supple and young like this dog, so she could see herself, from every angle.

Her breasts had "slumped" not fallen. The nipples were long and black; there was no hair around her nipples. Her abdomen was not flat. But it was not bloated, either. "Tummuch rich food I taking from that place down the ravine!" Her backside was broad. And it was her backside, whenever she had a man, that was love-tapped and massaged. "Good for fooping and bearing children," her husband used to say. When he'd said it, she had always said, "Don't listen to you!" Her legs were strong, and well-shaped. All the hours she spent walking to night classes, walking from kitchen to bedroom, from hallway to bedroom, from bus stop near the ravine to the community college where she had started and had dropped courses in Practical Nursing and Gourmet Cooking, but had been haphazard in her homework. "I just spending time, girl, just spending time! I muss look after myself." She looked at herself, long and critical, but then, with a pang of self-consciousness for the dog was staring at her. She pulled a long silk nightgown over her head, adjusting her left breast, holding it with tenderness and fitting it inside the bodice of the shimmering material. The dog was on its hind legs. A small, pink-coloured point of wet flesh had come out from under the dog's belly fur. It then grabbed her leg with its front paws. "Are you fooping me, dog?" She swallowed the Hennessy in one gulp, the dog still on her leg. "My God! Is this the kind o' dog you is? The kind o' dog they train you to be?" She tried to throw the dog aside with the fling of her leg; her slipper slid across the linoleum. She said, "Git! Git!" and stomped her foot and the dog fell back. "That's a good doggie." She flung herself on the soft queen-sized bed. Its accommodating springs took her weight, springs that had once been molested by the weight of two bodies, one heavier than hers, long long ago, the body of the man she was married to. She spread her legs, passed her hand across her nightgown to make space for the spread of her legs, and the dog sprang into that space.

"You son of a bitch!" she screamed.

She jumped down from the bed, holding the dog by the collar. She opened the door and the storm door and hurled the dog into the snow on the steps. She closed and bolted the door.

Shivering, she dialed Gerts.

"Goodnight," she whispered, more like a kiss than a whisper, as she poured herself another Hennessy against the night chill.

"What's your time? Let me set this alarm for tomorrow morning. What's your time?"

"Nine-thirty."

"Only that?"

"Miles and miles to walk…"

"What you saying, Gerts?"

"A poem."

"Who by?"

"Can't remember."

"I am cold cold, goodnight."

"Goodnight, my dear," Gerts said, but neither hung up.

She pulled three blankets up to her chin, and then over her head. "You still there, Gerts?" She thought she must look like a body, a corpse, that was the way she'd seen a corpse once in a television movie. She was whispering into the telephone, "So many hours and hours, the night still so damn young, Gerts!"

Old Pirates, Yes,
They Rob I

Won't you help to sing
These songs of freedom?...

I am in a small flat, in a guest room, as the landlady calls it; my stay being extended on the last day of the conference on Commonwealth Literature where I had been invited to speak; a conference of much whimpering and tongue wagging. I am alert in the early morning, sitting in bed close by a half-open window hearing a voice thin as a razor blade join Bob Marley's plaintive voice, two voices that come up from the outdoor car repair garage that sits to the east of this house of small flats, a car clinic atop underground parking places; one of the voices being an old recording of Bob Marley singing "Redemption Song." I feel sad to hear Bob Marley's voice and the thin voice of the mechanic working in the garage. I feel Marley's song, as I sit wrapped in bedclothes, is a personal chastisement,

Won't you help to sing
These songs of freedom?...

I hear the banging of wooden mallets on the metal rims of car tires; and the sound of car tires being rolled around under the sun of the outdoor garage, striking the galvanized paling; the voices of the Jamaikians below the window, their hands slick with thick car grease and oil from rummaging in the bowels of the engines; and the slamming of car doors, and the mechanic singing along with Bob Marley's strident, screeling voice

> *… old pirates, yes, they rob I,*
> *sold I to the merchant ships…*

And then the mechanic talking to two men in police uniform, the two of them getting out of their black car. The light on the top of the car is moving around in a slow red circle of menace; and one of the two police inquires, "What you know about who's up there?" I hear danger in the policeman's question as one of the mechanics looks up above ground to the window in my direction, a man I had said hello to and given the nod to. Looking back down to the ground, he replies to the police, "Me nah-know, man!"

This mechanic's one of those who had been brought here as a child to live in this neighbourhood of Brixton, and on the night I had arrived, with his hands and face smeared with the thick oil drains from crank cases, he had extended his hand in brotherliness. *Brotherly love,*

my arse! I had said in my Barbadian heart of snobbery.
Not in this world. Ma-fucker! – hearing "Bredder! Breth-
ren!"; making me think not of here and the hostilities of
this place, but of the silver sea, and of coconut palm
trees, giving me a stillness of mind for a moment, but
then again the calypso man Bob Marley's voice was in
my ear… sadder now, painful in its rebuke, rising in its
indignation at my measured silences, my day-to-day
refusal to help in any way that might mean physical risk.
I could hear the mechanics down below in the outdoor
shop now singing in tandem,

> … *how long shall they kill*
> *our prophets;*
> *while we stand aside and look…*

"Who's in there, that place?" a policeman says.
"Me no business with who lives up there, sah!"
"We need to know who is slipping and sliding, who
comes and goes these days."
"Me say, me nah-know, suh!"
But I know the stories of recent days in the newspa-
pers, I have seen the thick headlines in black, with photographs in colour, headlines that have reproduced the
anger and the blame, and the blood pouring down the
faces of black people… "the black English"… while I
passed the time of those evenings sitting silent in front

of the television set, hearing the BBC giving *Inglun* a bad name on the "whirl-news," hearing Big Ben banging in the background, hearing the national anthem, *God Save the Queen*, played before and after the news like the grace that was said before and after our island meals, voices that used to seduce us, my mother and me; voices that I had been schooled to; but now, in her letters posted from Barbados, my mother says, as often as she says grace, "Thank God you wasn' foolish enough to say you emigrading to go up-in-there, in Inglun, in preference to Toronto, a more better place for black people to find employment… even though the damn money so-blasted small!"

Now, this morning in this Brixton flat, having said my small piece at the conference, which was not a word of peace but perhaps could even have been taken in these electric times as a word of incitement, at least an incitement more than I had intended, I wonder where this mechanic below had spent those fiery nights. And who had stood with him in the singing of "songs of freedom." And who had helped him through the dark burned-out alleys of this city flowing in rivers of blood. And who it is who is needed now to help him find his way, as another kind of *help* is being threatened by the police who are hovering close by his side.

I hear the old elevator in this house of flats shudder to a stop. Another shudder tells me the door is open. The door closes. The closing sounds like a bullet fired into a cloth pillow. Or, into a man's chest. I can hear the elevator going down, down… as up comes Bob Marley again, pleading to the two mechanics and to me to answer the call; to be counted; to "… help to sing these songs of freedom." The plaintiveness in Marley's high-pitched voice seems more urgent and accusing. And, given my natural inborn and bred gift for caution, or more accurately, my well-nurtured airs of decorum, my need to always stand aloof from the crass abrasions of condescension and *ma-fucking* rage, I feel deeply the touch of danger, the cold hand; and I hear the policeman's voice again; inquiring, as he takes a warning, threatening tone, "Who doing what here?" drowning out the softer-voiced men who are working through the resurrecting clatter of car tires and metal rims.

Suddenly, it is cold; I am shivering; I am very lonely. More than lonely, I am alone. Fear clutches me. I do not know anyone in the yard, in the shop, in this house, in this neighbourhood. The two policemen are in their car, coming round to the front door. Their End-of-Times light on the roof is spinning and I anticipate one of the policemen will draw his gun, and will be standing close enough to me so that I am smelling his breath, while his gun is in my belly, and his voice, which sounds like a shout far out from sea comes to me over the waves: "You. What you doing here?"

"Me say, me nah-know, sah!"

This man and his kin, my brothers in a complicity by complexion, living here in Brixton, living here since being a boy; anger and hatred has raged all his nights, running through him like a cane fire – *Everywhere, everything burn down… Only ashes leff-back. Duss to duss. Ashes to ashes* – always on edge, in his small clinic for cars, bringing back to life punctured tires, the wheels of travel back into place; this man who had spoken with me briefly, spoken of danger; and the police and "skinhead" boys who wear tight-fitting trousers, with black boots whose pointed toes are implements of war, reinforced with lead, made on a blacksmith's anvil, to disfigure a black immigrant's face. I am absorbed for a moment in the lilt made in my mind by a litany of battles fought on the anvils of these island grounds: Bannockburn, Hastings, the Battle of Culloden, Naseby, Touton, Stamford Bridge and Stalling Down… bound as I am by a responsibility of blood to this newest history, these latest chapters of how and what the piratical are doing: the Riots of Notting Hill and Notting Hill the Riots again, the Riots of Brixton, Toxteth, Handsworth, the Riots of Bradford, Leicester and the Riots of Leeds…

Through the whole of this kiss-me-arse week of conferencing, I have been here walking these Notting Hill streets, through the whole of this time of tedium, these Commawealth Conferences, speaking and reading aloud

all sorts of such shite in the Reading Rooms of the fack-
ing Commawealth Institute… in all of this time I have
never stepped out in the streets to bloody my nose, to
brave the boots of these old robber pirates and their off-
springs, and by so doing to help *sing these songs of freedom*… and as I accept the accusation implied in that cry
for aid and help, I am scrambling into my underwears,
and my shirt pressed so fine and my tie, my university
blazer, and my Burberry, preparing myself to duck out
down the back stairwell, the stairs smelling of wine and
wastage, each floor landing single-lit by a bare bulb, so
that I can make my exit through the heavy steel back
door that has no outside handle; no outside handle to
advantage the police or transient interlopers; and then I
am walking fast fast down the cluttered laneway, having
given the slip to the police who are at the front door
seated in their car scowling under the whirling red
apocalyptic roof light, coming out on to the main thor-
oughfare of Brixton Road heading in the direction of the
Brixton Underground to escape the nausea of guilt that
"Redemption" has poured upon me, "Redemption" that
is asking me, bluntly, in full sunlight, to my face, into my
ears,

> *How long shall they kill our prophets,*
> *While we stand aside and look…?*

I know I am going in the right direction. Before me is the same man who one day, and perhaps for all of these days of duss to duss, has been here preaching the Gospel of the Downfall of London Bridge, his voice hoarse and filled with pebbles from repeating his Gospeller's promise of damnation, to the city, to me.

"Repent, London, repent England," he is screaming. His pulpit is at his feet, a cloth hat, nine coins. Two two-pound bank notes.

He is standing today in his same footsteps, preaching, preaching for hours now.

"Repent ye, London and England. London Bridge is falling down."

He breaks into song:

> Falling down, falling down!
> London Bridge is falling down,
>   My fair lady...

"Down-down-down... man-against-man... down... and the children against their mother... father 'gainst step-father... Jesus-Christ-in-Heaven, London tumbling to the ground... repent ye..."

I go down into the Underground, to lose myself in this darkness of people, in this blackness, although the escalators are lit in a dim fluorescence, descending slow, steep, moving stairs through darkness, the living dark- ness of this Underground, deep into this unspeakable safety.

FOR ALL I CARE

She sits like a queen. Thick around the hips. Solid around her breasts. Thick and strong down to her long finger-nails. With her eyes closed, silent, taciturn, a woman sitting dead still in a wooden straight-back chair.

"Just studying my head, boy," she says to me, her son, her only child.

Her hair is white in the severe "part" that is so perfectly drawn, and the teeth of her large horse-comb, standing in the plaits of her hair, is made of tortoiseshell.

It is a Wednesday afternoon, the sun still strong through the jalousies in the Dutch-window, strong on the pages of my exercise book. GEOMETRY, capital letters printed on the maroon-red front cover of the book. Isosceles triangles, squares, and circles and whatnot squared to prove what needs to be proved in this book. She had asked me what these proofs are, and I have explained them to her, but when she tells her best friend, Mistress Gallup, about isosceles triangles and angles at 45 degrees, they both rest their wet mops in the buckets of soapy water that smell of disinfectant, the smell coming from the blue soap they use for scrubbing the floors of the Marine Hotel for tourisses, where they work.

They put their hands on their waists, and shake their heads in pride. They know, though they cannot explain to themselves, or to their neighbours, what degrees of 45 at an angle or isosceles triangles do to enrich their lives, but their instinct reminds them that the knowledge that is spoken in their presence is something to be proud of, something that they will always be proud to remind themselves and the entire village of, this blessing.

I am her young man of seventeen who reads and studies "big books," and books written in foreign languages, and I have exposed her to these important things: a circle within a square, isosceles triangles, and Latin. "Imagine!" my mother says to Mistress Gallup. "Imagine."

It is about fifteen minutes after three, on this Wednesday afternoon. In plaits, her hair looks like a dark brown centipede. She says she imagines the sound its centipede body would make if she were to stomp on it. Mother rips the comb, made from the tortoise shell of a land turtle, free to loosen her plaits. She taps the teeth of the comb hard against the top of the wooden table, picking up the rhythm of a popular calypso that the village is singing.

The comb is brown. The villagers call it a "horse-comb" because it is larger and stronger and more polished than an ordinary comb, with colours running through it like smears of blood. Sometimes, Mother will plant the comb in her black hair, and leave it standing in a thick tuft, like an agricultural fork left in the fields, left amidst rows of green sugar cane stalks. But now the tapping of the comb against the table makes the sound of large red lima beans falling into a white enamel bowl, a tapping that is slower now, a slow dirge march, meditative.

"Boy! The Book! Bring me my Bible!"

Her voice is made strong by a touch of sudden joy: it is "Swing Low, Sweet Chariot" joy.

"Yes, Tawm," she says, "coming, for to carry me home!" I take the Bible to her. The black leather cover is torn. The condition of her Good Book does not worry her, does not challenge her disposition, or her love of God. She lowers her voice. She places the Book against her breasts, and says, "God's voice, Tawm-boy!"

I stand apart from her with my foot between the door and the jamb, to prevent the door from closing, and watch her as she runs her hands caressingly over the pages of the Bible. And I listen to her as she holds the Book up over the white tablecloth she had woven by her- self, wiping it clean. With her left hand. She does many things using her left hand: combing her hair, adjusting her gold bangles and her gold necklace, tying her shoes, and slapping me across my face, to remind me that she is the "damn boss inside this damn house, small as it is, boy!"... though she is not left-handed. And talking out

loud to herself, and perhaps to her God, who, as the
Holy Ghost, she said was always with her…

"… and here I am thinking thoughts I thought was forgotten, these thoughts coming back to trouble me like
stains in a dress that wouldn't come out, no matter the
amount o' detergent that I use, and I use blue soap and
stain-remover and still the damn stain won't leave my
dress at all at all. Or, it could be a silk nightgown that I
am washing. No matter the material, no matter how hard
I rubbing-out the nightgown or the dress on the jucking-
board, no matter how long I leave the nightgown or the
dress soaking in the water with the blue soap… what
with all the things that I have on my mind, I was sure
sure that by now today, the fourteenth o' March, that I
would have-emptied-them-out from my mind, from my
memory, years ago…

   "… that boy out there, who I don't know what I am
going to do with, he getting to be a man, and I still feel
that I born him only yesterday, the way I have to feed
him, wash him, starch-and-iron his khaki school-uni-
forms, feed him his food that is nutritional. Barley
soup. Chicken two times a week. 'Specially on Sundays.
And beef-broth every Wednesday. Enough and regular.
Keep the chicken for special occasions. Birthdays and
Easter… not to mention Christmas. My God, how I

going manage? That boy out there going eat me out of house and land! But he is my child! My only child. A good child. I have to give him good food. And enough good food to hold all those damn difficult hard heavy books, the Latin and the Geometry books, which he tell me so hard to learn. But what is this Latin business? Why does a young boy, in this bright island, have to learn Latin for? After trying so hard to learn to be who he is in English? And talk like a white man? And speak like a white man? His teacher at Harsun College is a white man. So that when he talk, the Englishman who is his teacher, would understand what the hell he want to convey. He has to learn how to convey what he want to convey, from what he actually say…"

I stand outside the door, out of her sight, but following her whisperings. I see what she is thinking, and what she has been concealing from me. But it is her life, and I am just her son. She has the right to keep these feelings, these secrets from me. She does not feel the need, and has never been burdened by the weight of confession, to tell me what is in her thoughts. Here she is, sitting in her straight-back chair, in the four-o'clock afternoon sun, with the sun shining on her face, shining as if she has rubbed it with Vaseline.

"... that boy out there, he, like the rest o' we, have we-own way of expressing what we want to express. We have our own own way of speaking. In arguments. In speaking-out our guts. With the truths. Or explaining what in our hearts. Important things. But the thing is, the thing is, that we does understand what we say to one another. And the person to who we speak, he or she, understand what we are saying to them."

She has turned her rocking chair around to catch the weakening sun, to catch the softening rays dying on her face like moths, that dying sun a pale sepia pink. She looks younger with the sun on her face like this. It makes her look more beautiful, closed eyes, slightly pouting lips in full satisfaction with the sun caressing her face. "Let the sun shine in! Let it shine always. 'Specially on your face, boy!" But where I am standing, away from the open door to the front-house, there is a growing scab of cloud threatening the afternoon with rain.

"... because you don't know... you never know... nobody knows, since it is a private thing that I never broadcast 'til today. And I ask myself, Why today? Why pick today? This damn letter causing me to suffer insomnias, the whole night, just arguing with myself, all night long until this afternoon, my two lips been closed, suppressing... so I never whisper a word of it! That boy, outside there, with his head buried in the Latin and the Geometry... books that is so hard for his poor brains... day in day out I walking with this cross that I bear and can't escape the burden of, walking with this cross, sending him to Harsun College where the school fees so blasted high I could buy enough lengths o' lumber to build-on another roof pon this lil chattel-house we living in. Private lessons and extra tuitions. Preparing him to make something of his self. He reading. Reading. And more reading. And all I can say to explain my situation is: if you only had a father. I mean it. It is obvious that that boy out there have a father. Had. Else, how he would have born? What I mean is this: I know that I didn' fool myself concerning any immaculate conception. I not meddling with that!

"But his real father... that blasted man... with all his sweet talk... I blame myself. All I could say now, is that it serve me right! To let him take the advantage of me that he take. I paying now, for it. The price of my softness o' heart. And my transgressions. The price for being friendly towards that brute!...

"I will never... never ever, as long as I live... never, until the day God take me from this earth, until I dead, I will never forget that blasted man. But I keep my word to you, Father! And praise God... praise you Father!...

for helping me to keep my word. To never let that blasted man's name pass my two lips. Nor mention it inside this house. Nor divulge it, in the hearing of that boy out there!... so quiet out there? In all these years that pass. In all these years! From that Monday morning! When me and him was lock in that fight, that morning by the Stand-Pipe. Like two cocks. Ripping out their guts. Feathers. Drawing blood. Me and him. For the whole neighbourhood to see. And hear. Such a worthless public display. At the Stand-Pipe. The corner o' Flagstaff Road, where it touch the White Road... that stretch o' road, out the Front Road, where only... or mostly... the white people does live. And in full view of all the people. Black and white watching me and watching that bastard. Black and white. And laughing. The two o' we. A coloured man and a coloured woman. Fighting like shite! Pardon my language, Lord... fighting over the legal ownership of that boy... my first-born son... out there, doing whatever it is he doing... on the sly... I can't put nothing past him!

"From that day that he born, premature, I may as well tell you... from that Monday morning... right up to this day... seventeen years... thank you, God! For giving me the strength to not ever let that blasted man' name pass my two lips... neither in abuse, nor certainly not in praise either... that son-of-a-bitch... not one day... in seventeen years... have his name ever pass my two lips.

Seventeen years! Count them. One, two three… four-teen, fifteen, sixteen. And seventeen. Praise God…"

I hear her horse-comb hitting the table top. Dot-dot… dot-dot, her shaking her head from side to side; taking up an envelope, putting it back on the table in the intervals, in the spaces, the silences, between her words, between her whispering.

"… and from that Monday morning, when that blasted man and me had that tussle over you boy… deciding the rightful ownership of my child… that blasted man's name, never ever… never never never… not once!… that blasted man's name never pass my two lips. And I thank God for not causing me ever to be in a position to have to call his name. Or, to see his face. In person. Alive. I do not think either that I will be walking behind his coffin. Or visiting him in the Parish of Sin-Michael's Almshouse. Nor on his death bed, neither. But thank God… in the fifteen years that I married to Daddy, now my legal husband, my loving husband… your stepfather… I have never ever had the occasion, nor the inclination, to mention your father' name, Daddy treating you as if you is his own own son.

"But I would never forget that morning, that being a Monday, the whole of every Tom-Dick-and-Harry in this neighbourhood, the Marrish-and-the-Parrish watching. And listening. And screeling. And pulling at the boy. White people and black people, both. To hear the two o' we, and the mistress woman who say in his face, 'Oh God, you intend to brek-off the child' two arms? And tekking way the woman lawful child? Oh God, man, watch out! You holding the child wrong. You holding the child by the neck! But, this child belongs rightfully to the child' mother! This child is rightfully the mother-own. All you men, and your tom-pigeons!'

"When I hear them words leave that woman's mouth, my hatred for that son-of-a-bitch, all that bile, all that venom o' hate come right up inside my head… my blood boiling… and I aim the kick. Good good good… and blam! Right in his two balls. Blam! Another kick. And he bend over, pulling my child's two feet, holding my child round his neck… Blam! And he leggo my child… and my God, I just in time to catch my child from falling and cracking open his head on the cement and the rock-stone that the Stand-Pipe build with… on my feet… when he start fighting me, pulling me, a child that born before it was time for him to be born… premature… so small, so little, so fragile, so teeny, but such a beautiful child. Born, as they call it, a Caeseerian. I carry him round the neighbourhood, in my two arms, on a pillow.

For the first two months of his poor life. But that Monday morning... I aim the blow... good good good. My left foot. Blam! Clean in his two stones. Good God! I myself was sorry for him, afterwards, after I kick him. Blam! And two more. Blam! Blam!

"I never understand how he was able to walk straight upright after that! With only one ball. One testicle, only? A cheer went up, 'mongst the spectators. The biggest cheer went up from the women. The white women. The men just walk off. Black and white. Black and white. And the whole damn neighbourhood, in particular the women, laughing. And clapping. 'Yuh win! Yuh win, girl!'

"And that woman's words cause tears to come to my two eyes. Just to see how close I had come to being a guest to Her Majesty's Glendairy Prison... serving a life sentence... for murder in the first degree. But if that was the decision that God judge me by... as I was sure sure that God had put me in the position to execute that deadly blow, I would have serve my time, in complete complacency, as God's decision... the payment for my deed. Payment for what that blasted man do to me... getting me big with child... and then having the nerve to try to take-way my first-born child from me? My only child? That boy out there, with his head buried in all them books... the Latin, the Geography... pardon me. I mean the Geometry... the Histories of the Whirl, that he have to read every night, for homework. And those books so hard to read! I happen to take the chance to peep in one, one afternoon when he went to the WC. The big words turn my head! My head start to spin and get giddy giddy. I had to put down the book. That boy, outside there, sitting down, doing his homework, or whatever it is that he doing… perhaps, even listening to me talking… and I hope he isn't… that boy will, one day, crown my head… with a crown o' gold, and… before he lift my head…"

I can hear the knocking of my mother's horse-comb on the table; I can imagine how her mouth tightens, and her lips become thin as shop paper; the sound of the comb knocking, knocking, keeping the beat of a church song on the tablecloth, a revival song, a hymn of salvation and redemption, sung at her Monday night congregations, when the married women in the neighbourhood gather for Mothers' Union. Perhaps my mother meant to copy the beating of her horse-comb onto the white tablecloth, imitating steel drums and a rhythm which enters her blood like a pulse, calypso in constant beat… I imagine her sitting with her right hand at her face, this posture allowing the music to crawl over her body as she whispers aloud her secrets to herself, secrets she has already told one of her women friends, Mistress Gallup, secrets too tragic and too disturbing for the ears of her son. I do

not know why I think this. But I am accustomed to seeing Mistress Gallup and my mother whispering; and
then suddenly, a silence would fall between them. They
would throw glances in my direction. This is when they
are talking woman talk, as her whisper turns into a tune
I have never heard, words: "Old pirates, yes, they rob
I..." Perhaps she has heard this on the short-wave radio,
the radio station that interrupts the song to say, "This is
the BBC. Here is the news, from London... read by...";
and then she listens to the playing of "God Save Our
Gracious Queen." She knows all the words to this
anthem and can follow the instrumentation of cymbal,
kettle drum, trombone, and bassoon. Sitting at the
Dutch-window in the front-house, she told me one day
that, "I counted the number o' times they play 'God Save
the Queen' today! Guess homminy times, boy! Guess."
And before I could guess, she tells me the number, exu-
berant, proud and smiling, knowing that she has this
knowledge and I do not.

"Ten! Ten times, since the first time it play, at six
o'clock this morning. It wake-me-up! Ten times!"

In my dorm room at Harsun College, I listened to the
Latin Master ask me to translate *Hannibal Alpam trans-
gresserat cum impedimenta*. I told him the translation
was, "Hannibal and his army crossed the Alps on the

backs of elephants." He closed his eyes, opened them, blinked, and then he said, pointing to the boy on my left, "Next ass!"

"... there is things I wish I could explain to that boy. I wish I could disclose to him the circumstances of my marriage to Daddy, instead of to that blasted man, his real father, and the history of how he get to be living with me, fatherless with only a stepfather, my only son, Tawm! Out there, in the next room. Reading a book. Or lis'ning to me talking and pretending he not listening to me tell him about his patrimonies. Because these is things every boy should know... who father him? But for me to explain... how Daddy come to be my husband, making that boy out there his stepchild, Tawm! The name I give my only child. Yes, Tawm!... I hope God will not get vex with me for withholding, in all these seventeen long years, the patrimonies of my son's birth from him. Who else am I going to keep it from? And hold it from? If not from him? In all these seventeen years, his stepfather, who is more like a father to him, in the way he treats my son... and he too, I must say, have never degradated the sanctity of this house by calling that man's name, inside this house. Not once. And his name never cross my two lips in these seventeen years that pass. Not once. Not even when I am by myself. Alone. In this house. Not once.

"I sitting down here the whole day. The whole morning already gone! And Jesus God, here I am, at this dining table, with this envelope that the postman bring yesterday. And it is Wednesday already. And four o'clock gone! Time catch me, still sitting down here! With this tortoiseshell horse-comb, in my one hand. Whilst saying these things to you whether you here or not with your ears open wide... and this envelope. I don't know if you hearing my words. If you understand what I saying, cause I can't see your two eyes. Hearing things I wish I could tell you, face-to-face, and put you in a seat, 'side-o'-me, and make you siddown and listen to me, as your mother. Looking into your two eyes, the only proof that my words was reaching you. Reaching your heart. No escaping from the truth in my eyes, my eyes touching your eyes. And your eyes would be the only proof my words are touching your heart. I wish it was possible to discourse the things I went through, to you.

"But the two o' we hiding from one another. So, what is he seeing in all them big books, that he can't see in my words? And what, can he, as my child, pulled out of my womb, in a Caeseerian operation, bleeding in pain, cause he was born before it was his time to be born... what can he understand from what I am feeling, or thinking? My past? His present? Our present and past?

"So, I will remain ignorant. Or dumb. I will never understand one word that he is reading. In them books. Nor what he is suffering. In the silence. In the silence I been spreading over his life?

"Seventeen years o' secrets, and silence? But I already admit to that. I am repeating myself. I know there is reason enough for a woman to repeat herself. Poor people, 'specially women like me, have to repeat themselves. Is our only consolation. That boy, sitting down out there, in the shed-roof, should know everything about me, his mother. Well, not every everything...

"But seventeen long years? Carrying this heavy burden o' guilt? And, added to this, the heaviness of having to confess it? But, if he have to know... really have to know the truth, it can't come from my two lips. I can't confess it, act-by-act, to my son. To my own son? To my only son? What can I tell him about the man who got me pregnant? And the other one, that Canadian boy, the Sous-Chef... promising me to open a new life with him? Up in that cold country, Canada? Never mind he didn't succeed. But would my life be more better with him, up in Canada?

"So, you don't think I have reason enough not to let that bastard's name cross my two lips? To pronounce it? And in the hearing of that boy, out there fulling up his brains with foreign languages? All this Latin. All this Geometry. All this History about our beginnings. And such a terrible beginning, as he tell me, it was, that we had, in ancient times! In a different place! Born in one place. Tek from that place. Then, transported to a different place. With a stop-over in England... our Mother country! What kind o' Mother England was to me? Or is? And my God, in Africa? To live in England and in Africa, is the same thing as 'living at your aunt,' as we say, the worst thing that could happen to a child, particular a little girl, is to make her live at her aunt. Lots o' floggings. And little food. And the rest is unspeakable, as they say...

> *Nobody know the trouble I see,*
> *Nobody know the trouble I see...*

"Ghana, they say. According to our resemblance to that breed o' slaves... and they bring we here. If you was to ask me to tell you more than what the sum of two and two is; or anything more than the Pig-Latin language that we speak, if we want to hide what we say, the truth sometimes, from somebody... 'specially from the white people...

"'I ud-kay el-tay oo-yaa it-shay... and-a oo-yah o-nay...'

"Who else but we, born here, or who was drop-off here, from Ghana, would know this new language? Or even know it exist? So, I am left back in the dark, no longer able to speak the language of Pig-Latin, that I born speaking?

"Hey-haiii! I have to laugh! Here I am, sitting-down, looking at the envelope, all this time, using this high-faluting language, and I really don't know what the arse I am saying. Even in this. Talking every day in a language… and every day hearing it spoken-back to me, by that boy out there, and really and truly, if I am going to be honest, I don't know what the arse he says to me sometimes, when he talk to me in his greaty greaty English tones and accent… as if he is a white man! And as a consequence, he don't know what the hell I am saying to him, neither… "

My mother is still sitting in the front-house. I am in the back room, the shed-roof we call it, from where I can see the backyard with the chickens and the fowls, and the flies, and the WC. She is looking out through the Dutch-window. She can see the people passing in the road. I can hear the comments she makes on their dress, on the clothes they are wearing, on the way they look. If she could sprain her neck, and look towards the Hill, which lords itself over the valley and the Hill itself, she would see "the Atlantic Ocean!" I hear her husband, my step-father, say so, many times. He says it with pride, boasting; showing off; showing me his knowledge of the

History of Barbados, and the History of the Whirl. "The Atlantic is the sea that bring we here. From Africa. The sea that transport we here, in shit and ships, painted in doo-doo, across the Atlantic Ocean, boy!" And he leaves it at that, for me to drink-it-up, and digest it.

My mother continues to look through the Dutch-window at the people passing; and she turns her head to the right, and then, to the left, following them for the short journey, the short time they come into focus, at the right-hand corner of the window from the right, and then disappear in the left-hand side of the Dutch-window to the left, and then wiped out of the lens of her eyes… And she seems bored by this. To me, they all are dressed the same, and they walk with the same surrender, for they are late for their appointments: school or work; school or civil service. Teachers, perhaps. Chauffeurs.

And she quenches her boredom by turning her head to look at the chickens in her backyard. She looks at them, as I follow her gaze. She looks at them now that her taste is deadly. She has chicken or duck or young turkey on her mind, in the taste in her mouth. In the palate of her desire. And the thought of killing comes into her head. She tastes the flesh of chicken, boiled or roasted, in her mouth. She tastes the blood. A chicken passes closer to me, where I am standing at the door leading into the kitchen. I can hear the tapping of her horse-comb change its tempo; and its rhythm. Perhaps, she is knocking the horse-comb to the new rhythm of the chickens and ducks and the young turkeys who march in circles. The circles are surrounding her. Look! A cock. Young and fluttering his wings and bragging about his feathers that grow out of his body like golden flashes of manhood.

The sun has come out again. It adds glory and lust to the cock's body of horns and sex, practising his jumps on to the back of a hen. The young cock does not balance his desire on the back of the hen. And he falls off. But, now! Look! They are stuck together, for a short time, practising their balancing, and oh!… then losing it. And to me, they are now two, rolling in the afternoon dust in the backyard. The cackling of the cock's defeat increases. And the defeated fowl-cock surrenders. The cock is not able to jump on the hen, and still hold his balance. Then, the fluffing of his wings and feathers. My mother is thinking, I imagine, of the performances of the cock and the hen; of their gentleness, and their ignorance of the scales, balancing their two fates, hanging over their heads. She is no longer thinking of crunching their bones, and sucking out their eyes.

I am suddenly aware that the house is quiet. Quiet. Still. Still as if the chickens and the ducks and the young turkeys cackling in the backyard have now turned into the men and women who pass her, from the left-hand, and the right-hand, as she sits, in all this silent time, at the opened Dutch-window.

The quietness gobbles up the unmusical tapping of the horse-comb that she plays with, on the wooden table covered by the white cloth. I remember how I had watched her, patient, stitch by stitch, including the misses and the anger that stayed with her, as her large fingers had worked over the delicate white cloth.

Now, the tapping replaces the stitching. The tap... tap... tap... tap-music that she makes with the tortoise-shell hitting the top of the table. The way I make music begins and ends with the one finger plucking on the one-stringed Stradivarious of the man who lives next door. But I know enough about music, and from listening to the neighbour's Stradivarious, to understand the manner in which my mother slams the tortoiseshell on the table top, just like she slams the "seeds" in a Friday night domino game, after the stories about the Sinner Man. I know it is nothing more than her way of concealing her anger.

I know that she will transfer this anger to the way she kills "this bloody bird," her word for a chicken about to be killed. She will hold the "bloody bird" by its neck; tight; as if she is holding a child's rattler. And with two swings, the "bloody bird" is just the fluttering of a weakened heart. And then, she cleans her hands, spotted in blood, on her white apron that hangs down to her shins. She has been sitting at the Dutch-window, for hours now. And I am hearing the crunching of chicken feet and their cackling, and the music that their cackling makes: the cackling of hunger; the currying and fluffing of their beautiful colours, like flashes of gold on this Wednesday of dying sunlight. She is paying more attention to the chickens and fowls than to the envelope or the people entering from the right and from the left in front of her Dutch-window.

I am wondering about that envelope, that Griffoot the postman brought yesterday. And wondering about all the things she is telling me. That she won't admit she's telling me.

A voice comes through the short-wave radio. It says, "The time now, is exactly four-thirty, Greenwich Mean Time." And I wonder which "bloody bird" parading in my mother's backyard will lose its neck, on this humid, cackling, Wednesday "bloody" afternoon. I can, already in my mind, smell the aroma of boiling chicken, rising soft like the first kisses of morning mists; and I can taste the chicken boiling in the aluminum saucepan. This saucepan for boiling things reminds me always of the helmet of a Roman legionnaire; and "my God!," as my mother would say, imagining the sweetness that lies within the legionnaire's helmet, along with the sweet potatoes, and pulped eddoes and pigtails. All this is boiled-down in a bed of long-grain Indian rice. And fresh hot peppers. "To put a lil kick in this chicken stew, boy."

"... oh Lord, only if it was Friday! And not still this Wednesday afternoon! I could throw into this chicken stew some cloves; some hot nigger-peppers; some fresh ones, picked straight offa the tree; some onions; and some sprigs o' fresh thyme that I growing in the backyard; my God!... and by the time she bake and I throw a little Mount Gay Dark Rum all over she, and pour some lard-oil over she!... oh my God, boy! Look out!

"But today is only Wednesday! Overcast. A sad, dark, lonely lonely day!... this Wednesday! As if something bad is going to happen.

"This Wednesday is more like a Friday... good Friday! Even with the sun still out..."

I am still listening in the shed-roof, the small room off the kitchen, to the sound her horse-comb is making... tic... tic... tic... tic... tack... trying to find out what she is composing in her mind with the brown blood-smeared shining tortoiseshell... if there is an actual song she is composing and playing. Perhaps she has fallen asleep in the heavy humidity that is bathing her black silken skin. Perhaps she is not singing at all, for the door to the front-house is now shut. I am hearing now a humming song, with some words intermittent, sung by her; those she remembers. Perhaps, she isn't singing at all. And that what I am now hearing is my own imagination displacing a melody that the afternoon's warm, four-o'clock humidity gives birth to. Perhaps, the sound is that of the tortoiseshell. And she is punctuating her words and her imagination and my interpretation of her words in my mind, as if I am in a dream. Imagine. Perhaps I am dreaming. Dreaming from the moment I hear the tic, tic... tic... toc... beaten on the wooden table, made for her, by the man who lives next door, who plays the Stradivarious guitar that has one string, with one finger.

She looks to me like one of those women who comes alive on the pages of a library book in which she had read about indenture and reaping cotton and planting short pieces of sweet potato and sugarcane cut expertly by her and by hundreds of others whose names she does not remember now... women, were they called Sugars? Dots? Sweetness? Girly? Negro? Lil Nig? All of whom, her own mother and the mothers of all the young girls like her, were born and raised in the plantation tenements. Yes! It is the same women. Right there in the book. "It's in the book!" somebody said. "It's in the book!" Indenture-women. Indentured as slaves. "They bring we here, from where we was. The same thing they put we through. Right there in that book. *The Crossing*. That was the name of that book. But I start-out telling you bout the lickings and the whips, cut fresh from the tamarind tree and still green... whap!... whap!... whap! Whap!"

She looks at the envelope lying on the table, where it has been since yesterday. She was sitting right here, just as she is now, when she heard the ring of the bicycle bell. The rain started to come down. It was warm. Like the sea when it touches the skin, first thing in the morning. It is the afternoon of Tuesday. The rain falls in thin drops, like water poured through a sieve, made with small holes. My mother remains at the Dutch-window. The rain drops become warmer; and heavier. And they cause her to put her hands to her throat, as if she is about to strangle herself, holding them there. And then she uses them to close her bosom and her neck from the strange draught which strikes her neck and her breast.

Ring-ring!... ring-ring... ring! Ring! Announcing rings. She knows this ringing. She has heard it before; many afternoons. It is familiar. The afternoon and the rain falling, and the tricky colour of the skies above her head, above the trees, above the telephone wires that had just brought her the time..."Four-thirty. Grennitch Mean Time," is so confusing this morning. "But it is not morning! Is afternoon!... morning gone long-time." Still, she is not sure of herself; sure, even, of recognizing the sound of the bicycle bell.

The grandfather clock is ticking. The rain is heavy on the trees. Mango, avocado pear, tamar-ind, and paw-paw are now all drenching the neighbours passing, and who walk under them. They are getting wet, two times: once from the trees; once more from the rain itself. The rain has painted the trees in the same colour. Into a rich, painful green. And the bicycle bell is insistent as if it were announcing some tragedy, or more rain to come later in the evening. The bicycle bell searches for the person for whom the *ring-ring! Ring-ring* is intended. The bicycle bell ignores the ominousness that its silver, nerve-sting-ing intends. The grandfather clock, just behind her... tick... tock... tick tock... is ticking sad in a hollow made of silence, as if it were announcing an unwelcome visitor, perhaps a friend or former friends or enemies, and especially that one person, "that blasted man. But why welcome him?..."

She flings the shutters of the Dutch-window back. The The afternoon is exposed to her now.

Ring-ring! Ring-ring! Ring-ring!

"My God! Griffoot, the postman," she says. "Griffoot come already? My God. It is five o'clock, already? Griffoot delivering letters already." As if by arrangement, the grandfather clock strikes five times. It is a mournful greeting of time and postman. And the rain is coming down, harder. With the jalousies of the Dutch-window thrown open; she exposes herself and her thoughts, to the elements. And to Griffoot.

"Five o'clock! The whole day gone, so early?" she says. The rain is driving out of the skies, piercing through the avocado pear trees and the paw-paw trees, and the mango trees, onto her exposed face. She sees the Raleigh three-speed bicycle. It is painted green. Yes, it is Griffoot. The postman. He is walking towards her, holding his bicycle with his right hand, getting drenched, stepping gingerly into broadening pools of water, picking out the few drier sections of the path and stretches of sheltered grass leading to the front door to walk on. He has not seen her yet. The rain is even heavier now. He rings his bicycle bell again. *Rrring-ring! Rrring-ring! Rrring-ring-rrrrubg-rrrrring!* The two jalousies of the Dutch-window begin to bang in the wind with the rain. Griffoot can see her now. She has seen Griffoot.

"Griffoot? Why you out in the rain making such a racket, with that damn bicycle bell, on my premises for?"

Mr. Griffoot has to walk gingerly through the deepening pools of rainwater that have gathered on the grass and in the gutters at the side of the house. He is dressed in khaki trousers, khaki shirt, khaki jacket with silver buttons that run up to his neck; and three smaller ones at the sleeves. And a matching khaki cap, with a peak; similar to the caps worn by private liveried chauffeurs who wear uniforms. Griffoot wears two black plastic clips round his ankles, to protect his brown shoes. His shoes are sopping wet. He puts the clips on round his ankles, in a heavy rain like this, to prevent his trousers from catching in the chain. The chain is greased thick with "car-grease." Griffoot holds a letter in a brown envelope under his khaki jacket to protect its contents from the rain and from the eyes of any malicious neighbour, in case. He knows neighbours indulge in malice. After shaking off the water on his jacket, his shoulders and his sleeves, he hands her the brown official-size envelope.

She holds her face up to the rain, like a child, to let the cool water wash her face. She does not sing as children do in the rain.

Griffoot waits at her window.

"Girl, how are you?" he says.

"I here, boy," she says.

"Letter for you. It look important."

"Who writing me this important-looking letter? Eh, Griffoot, boy? You know who it from? Eh, Griffoot, boy? You know who writing me?"

"Guvvament, it look like. OHMS, girl."

"On Her Majesty Service?"

"How you know that?"

"On the envelope."

"Her Majesty?"

"Or His Majesty's."

"Guvvament it look like. OHMS, girl!"

"What this is now, nuh?"

"Read it, and you'll see. I going down the Hill… Incidentally, you have anything hard? A lil Mount Gay…? Even, if necessary, a glass o' ice-water?"

"But Griffoot! How you mean… if I have a glass o' water?"

"Read the letter good, girl. I going down the Hill…"

"Lean-up the bicycle 'gainst the house… whilst I look for a drink for you. If I can't get you a drink, at least, I can afford a glass o' ice-water…"

"One thing I can't understand… why poor coloured people like we, love to write summuch damn letters! Only giving me a lot o' blasted work. 'Specially when the rain falling so hard. And wetting-up my blasted clothes… and wasting all this paper… and giving me all this hard work. Incidentally, how Tawm?"

"He back there like always… in the back-room… in the shed-roof, behind that door… reading his Latin, and other Ancient things, like the Histories of Ancient places, if you please! Or, so he tell me. So he tell me…"

She chooses a crystal shot-glass. She pours it to the brim.

"Emm! Emm-emm!" Griffoot says, the drink hitting his palate as he clears his throat, anticipating the satisfying strength of the Mount Gay dark rum from Daddy's decanter. It is Mr. Griffoot's usual reaction when he drinks dark rum. She serves it with a matching saucer, on a white napkin that has white flowers and squares knitted into it, like her tablecloth. She made the napkin herself. She hands Griffoot a second drink, "his gay drink," as she calls it, whenever he passes; whenever he rings his bicycle bell three times, announcing his arrival, whenever my mother is sitting at the window, looking like she is about to sing out. Griffoot and Stepfather sing in the choir, bass and tenor of the Sin-Matthias Ang-lican Church by-the-Sea, down the hill, through Brit-ton's Hill, down, down, down to the small church, on the beach, looking out to the sea.

Griffoot wipes his mouth with the back of his hand. It is his left hand. He straightens his jacket; he shakes the rainwater from his cap; he brushes off the excess water from his jacket; from his trousers, from his cap, all with his left hand. He holds his right arm stiff like a man who has been wounded. He then slaps his clothes, as if he were beating a child. He does not have any children.

He takes his hat off. And beats it against the khaki postman's bag that contains letters and parcels. His trousers and his shirt and his jacket are all made from the same material, including the cap, of strong brown khaki. He is tidy once again. And he smiles with her, when he swallows the last sip of the rum, and promises to stop, when he passes tomorrow, if she is at the window, if he has another important-looking letter, stamped OHMS on the back of the envelope, and with her address on the other side.

And Griffoot walks back to the road. He stops. Turns around. Rings the bicycle bell, *rrring-ring!… rrring-ring!…* like a final greeting; and jumps on the saddle, making himself comfortable on the leather seat. When he turns the corner, he is still waving. He free-wheels down the Hill, into the village.

She punches the index finger of her right hand into the brown official envelope. The one she has been toying with. It is the same way she punches her hands into the guts of a flying fish or a chicken to pull the guts clean out the body. She pulls out the white type-written paper. It is folded two times over. And she flattens the type-written letter out on her right leg, just above her knee. The letter is one sentence long. "The purpose of this letter is to inform you that…"

That was yesterday. And now she sits, sad, holding that same envelope in her hand. She puts it down. It is raining again. The rain is falling light. It seems to make her more sad. She is alone. And lonely. Her loneliness creeps into her body, just like the chill of the morning dew. But on this late Wednesday afternoon, just as the dusk falls, the light rain has stopped, and the dew has turned to humidity. And then this heaviness, this loneliness, this sadness, which has a taste like strong dark rum, has come upon her.

She takes the crystal glass from the table. She lifts it to her mouth. The glass catches the weak light of the afternoon. The sun is dying. Sliding into the peaceable waves. She can see the waves from her window.

Such afternoons she sits in this same chair watching this same sun, the size of it, the weakness of it. From the silence of the dying sun, she has seen many things. She places her hand over her breasts, to make herself tidy.

There is no one for her to talk to now. Things around her are changing into shapes that she cannot define. Mango trees, paw-paw trees, golden-apple trees, avocado pear trees, and ordinary trees surround her, and with the fleeing of shapes there is the new silence of sadness that surrounds her like the lingering smell of the Mount Gay Rum. She moves her hands searching for something, searching not with her hands; nor with her eyes; and in fact she does close her eyes, and her hands; first her left hand moves over the tablecloth, and then her right hand follows that hand, and then she stops. Abruptly. She finds what her hands are searching for. The envelope.

It has turned surprisingly cold. Almost chilly. But the afternoon though dying is still not close enough to spread its deathlike coldness over a piece of paper, over a piece of brown paper, with OHMS printed just above her name: Mrs. G. Jordan...

"All night I thinking of this letter, come too late for me, now that he dying. But not for the boy. And now I told that boy what I promise the Lord I would never say... that blasted man's name. Why now? Why now? But now it's out of my hand. It's up to the boy now.

"Tawm! Tawm! Tawm!"

Her eyes are closed. She is moving her head from side to side. She lets out a deep moaning sound. She moves her head like this, when she has a toothache, which makes her cry "rivers o' tears," as she calls it: shaking her head from side to side, shaking her body with her eyes squeezed shut.

"Tawm-Tawm! I know you standing there listening to every word I breathe!"

She is stomping her foot, her right foot, on the sand spread on the floor, to help keep it clean. The grains of sand make a grating noise.

"Come, boy!"

She pulls the letter from the envelope, furious now, and waves it at me. I can see across the top: Sin-Michael Almshouse for the Indigent.

"Seventeen years too late!... and in all this time the blasted man coulda been dead. Shoulda. For all I care..."

SO?

And then I draw circles on her nipples, with my index finger; and then I touch sweet velvet, silky and fresh as an oyster... and the blood starts pumping through... and I am counting the notes in the violin that Mendelssohn is playing... and I drop off into a dream... of sea water and sun and the wind fleeing over the Atlantic Ocean; coming to me, on the island: waves coming in, slow and sure. And she is nearly there, approaching on the waves of her own arrival; and then...

"Oh!"

... and then, she whispers for me to take it easy. "Please," she says, "easy." Her voice is a whispering. "Easy..." This is the second time now, making it seem that at this moment, she is not sure. Fear is in her voice. And her voice comes in soft shudders... one after the other; as if she is not sure that she can carry the explosion that is in her body, like "rushes" that increase and build inside her body her body...

"No!"

... and I rest. And I think of how else I can make her happy. While I wonder, she is shivering: pulling her body away... determined to regain her freedom... and in the midst of this, her question, "How would I make love to you, if I was making love to you?" Her question is like a dream: but I am not dreaming now.

I am in the chilly sitting room. And she is dressed in white; a ghost, in her long cotton nightgown, transparent enough to make my eyes see, easily, what I should not see. It fits her long like her wedding dress.

Her legs are outlined, marked out in their sturdiness in this mid-February winter light; and her breasts are heaving; and getting heavier; and Mendelssohn is a whisper now. I hear her whisper...

"Yes!"

I am not imagining that I am hearing the whisper.

"Yes."

It is a cold, chilled appeal and confession...

"Yes."

I was... I was... one time...

Mendelssohn is...

"Please... be patient... easy, please..."

Mendelssohn is soft like the pads that control the vibrato in a muted trumpet.

"Oh, Jesus Christ!" she screams.

So? So? And the trumpet spits the question out. So? So? The trumpet is muted. The question becomes philosophical. And its place is taken by the turbulence of the drum, beating, beating, coming from being just the provider of the beat and the rhythm, and now, it is in the forefront of this blues music that I am hearing; into the ferocity of laying down the beat. The tenor saxophone has taken over from Miles: and Miles has surrendered and is keeping time, beating it out by the tapping of his shoes. All this time, I have turned my back to the audience. If I ever had an audience. I have no audience. There is no audience to witness this. The tenor saxophone is in a rage. Coltrane's notes...

I am at this time, standing beside the Juliet window, in the sitting room, swallowed up by the lamenting muted trumpet made more sad and sullen by the tenor saxophone which takes it on the same journey, but in thicker woods and into trees growing in marshes with long branches, strong and thick as rope to fit the neck, in a lynching.

The trumpet is replaced by the tenor saxophone that Coltrane is playing, beating a different time, faster than the trumpet that had already whispered the slow sadness in the music, and had hinted at the indifference buried in the one-syllable word, So! and had hinted at the theme: "pahm-pam... pahm-pam... pahm pam... pashm-pam... pahmm-pam... pahm-pammm" – and I can hear the sound of the keys that touch the felt and the metal of the saxophone, which is swifter, and which gives a new measurement of time and space to the music. It makes my heart beat faster; and my blood pump thicker than the lackadaisical pace of the blues for the trumpet's own seductive repetition of desire; and with the triplication of this desire, with its minor keys. It paints a picture, for me, defining want and hunger. It brings to my mind, a canvas: the icon of a man in a shack in the Deep South, singing "Carry Me Back to Old Virginny."

The cold wind is coming through the white sheer curtains at the Juliet window. It hugs me round my shoulders. And soon, I am dozing off. I am alone in the large house, in the sitting room; soaked in the perfume of pink Japanese flowers, whose leaves are soft; soft as her nipples; and as beautiful.

I put my head against the bathroom door, and imagine that the sound I am hearing is the hissing of mist born of the hotness of the water. The sound of mist. Mist rising from beneath the closed door. I can hear the water from the shower as it forces through the pores in the shower head. I know that it is tilted to give the body… in preference, the body of a woman… powerful, satisfying steaming waterfalls. I listen. My head is against the door. I keep it there for a long time, the steam flowers up from the bottom of the door. I hear the woman's voice. Or I think I hear it, like a cry for help; coming, coming through the mist, and it rises, just like the top registers of the muted trumpet, the instrument at Miles Davis's lips.

The woman's moaning voice slips under the bathroom door.

"Yes, yeah-esss... Yes!"

The woman's voice is in a higher register now.

"Yes!"

I cannot see her. I do not know the cause of her cry. The bathroom door is shut.

Her voice is quickening. Is higher. Triplicatingly higher. As high as the lightning touch of the keys of the tenor saxophone, in its deep, sensual sound.

"Yes..."

It sounds like exhaustion. And then, there is silence.

There are no mists now. Death has swallowed them up.

"So?"...

THEY NEVER TOLD ME

I am getting old. And I hate it. I use swear words to stem the silent flow of years that overtake my actions, and even the flow of my speech. My first recognition of this malady of old age is the stumbling, and the climbing of stairs. And after many trials, the stammering to find the word that does not come easily into my mind, and that remains on the tip of my tongue. And they never told me how to be cool and decent about this slowing down of speech; the lengthening struggles to find the correct word, remembering it until I match the thought to the written word itself... the fading of faces, the disappearance of names from the faces that my eyes move over, like an usher's flashlight in a crowded cinema; and from the pages of names in my pocket diary. I am old. But I hide it. I hide my fear of old age; and my shame of it. I do not want to get old; do not want to be recognized; to be greeted by old friends, precisely because they are old; or, to be pointed out by a smiling young woman, with her eyes, and a nod, and a smile, that illustrates her question, and her concern, "Would you like my seat, sir?"

But I take the offer and take her seat; and my indignation swells, and smells like stale perspiration. I take the seat. I am very close to this young woman as she stands up. I can see the thin outline of her panties through the summer-thin dress. I become ashamed of myself. Of my desire. And I want to scream my indignation out, to everyone on this crowded bus, "Do I look so old to you?"

But shame and reality keep my lips shut.

And when I return to my house, two hours after my encounter with the kind young woman, I confront myself in the small unframed, rectangular glass over the white washbasin. The washbasin is made of smooth white enamel. The small bathroom is painted white. The paint shines. There are large brown bottles and a damp washcloth in the sink; and bottles of pills for headache, and pills for earache; and pills to pacify the cough that rumbles in my chest; and pills for head colds. And pills for losing weight; large pills, colourful pills, pills that I have left untouched, left in a bulbous green bottle. And then a round tin, flat like a puck slapped around in a hockey game. Kiwi Black Shoe Polish! And around the tin are the words, "noir, kiwi, black, kiwi, noir, kiwi, black, kiwi." I had not known that "kiwi" was another name for "black." I turn the catch, the little metal wings on the tin. "Water resistant. Leather nourishing." And round the diameter of the tin is the reassurance: "By appointment to H.R.H. the Duke of Edinburgh. Makers of shoe polish." The picture of a kiwi bird is drawn in yellow.

As I twist the catch, the full power of the shoe polish strikes my nostrils; and I dig my middle finger deep into the thick, silky blackness, moving my three fingers covered in the black soil of thick shoe polish over my face – I think of Negro minstrels, and of white men who wanted to turn themselves into black men. The hand that holds the black shoe polish is black. And nervous. And shaking in the horror of the act I am committing; turning myself into a black-face black man; while all I wanted to do was to slick my hair with black shoe polish, to make myself look sleek and younger; to make young women stop getting up to offer me their seat. I want to look young. I rub the black shoe polish into my skin. I look at my reflection. And I see the laughing face of a man. The face of Al Jolson. The face of a white man who sang like a cantor who is Negro, whose hand is black, and I imagine myself singing a song written by a white man, by Stephen Foster pretending to be a down home country boy black man,

> *Way down upon de Swanee Ribber,*
> *Far far away,*
> *Dere's whu my heart is turning ebber,*
> *Dere's whu de old folks stay…*

I am an old man still, and I am mouthing the words of this song; and my back takes on the shape of an old man moving to the slow beat of the song. My back is bent. The song overcomes me. My lips are large; and red. My eyes droop. My hands shake. I am Al Jolson. I am singing the minstrel blues,

> *Way down upon de Swanee Ribber,*
> *Far far away,*

and my face is by appointment to H.R.H. the Duke, and I feel comfortable with my new darkness, and I move my body slow. And I dance, and I laugh and my teeth become pearly white, and my eyeballs lose their pupils; and are now completely white. And I am rocking from one side to another side. And my voice has become deep, and I roar with laughter at my antics.

I sometimes come to my home and climb the forty-seven steps to this bathroom, and after I close the door behind me, I find I'm lost in my head, I've forgotten completely why I climbed those steps. So I retrace my forty-seven steps, counting out loud their number. The count becomes everything, mindful that one false step will send me hurtling down to smash myself against zero, the bronze panel in the front door; and then, I will have to rouse myself and re-climb and re-count the forty-seven steps, and enter the bathroom a second time… and then try to remember why I had entered it the first time. But now it comes back to me. I had wanted to get a tissue of white Kleenex to polish my reading glasses with so I could see *whu my heart is turning ebber...*

In the bathroom, I look at my blackened hair, not so black as I had wanted it to be, and I turn the tin of shoe polish over, and I see it is a tin of Canadian shoe polish made at the Kiwi Polish Company (Canada) Limited, in Hamilton, just a few miles west of Toronto; and this closeness, like family, makes the black paint on my face more acceptable. I like being black-faced. In safety and security beneath the "black, kiwi, noir" of my new complexion, behind the mask that is painted black on my face. I can now wallow in the peace of being lost in a place where I will take a seat beside a young woman, where I will inhale her alluring perfume; and when the bus stops, enjoy the touch of her arm, and wonder if at my age – which nobody knows for certain – if her sweet, soft arm, and the whiff of her auburn hair against the blackened, curled hairs on my unshaven chin, could ever reawaken that dormant, once sweet sensuality which... "dream on, old man!..." might come alive, stand as erect as the first bursts of spring flowers, with me now travelling in peace; buried deep in the deeper tranquility of forgetfulness.

Riding up and down on a bus, the Rosedale route down to the waterfront on Sherbourne Street. I even stop and get off at the large LCBO liquor store. And buy a mickey of rum, fifteen-year-old El Dorado Rum, made in Demerara. And back on the bus, I sneak a sip from the shaking bottle, caused by the hard driving over a broken pot-holed road, and caused by the strength of the rum. I hold the bottle under my winter coat. Nobody sees me. Nobody looks at me. Nobody cares. I am an old black man with my face painted black at the back of the bus.

And the bus turns around, going north from the waterfront along this same Sherbourne Street where it touches Queen Street East; past the multitudes of bums and beggars; and the homeless; and drunks; and no one knows me. I have become one of them. No one has to be kind to me, to offer me a seat. I can hum. I can sing, under my breath, like Al Jolson, the whole entire song…

> *Way down upon de Swanee Ribber,*
> *Far far away,*
> *Dere's whu my heart is turning ebber,*
> *Dere's whu de old folks stay…*

I have to admit, however, with some embarrassment, and more shame, sitting on the rough-riding bus, that the call of the bathroom has become urgent oftener now and no longer do I have the urge that I used to have to pacify my urge to pee. With a mind that no longer distinguishes amongst faces and nor does it recognize one address from the other, a mind that does not place a face against a telephone number, I watch my own sloughing off of habits of cleanliness, I watch my own deterioration, my own incapacities; the increasing difficulty to unscrew the cap of a plastic bottle; trying to unscrew the cap of the gin bottle; reaching up to take frozen food from the refrigerator; or to accept the offer of space in a line-up at the cinema; and beneath it all, there is my increasing urge to pee, to empty, to void myself. Would those who offer me such consideration want to help me pee? To help me into the void? Full of good-willed unawareness. I resent all such gestures, especially when they come from young women. Not many women my age express these pleasantries. No woman of my age has ever offered me her seat. I presume it is because we are in the same boat, a boat that more and more refuses to float.

In the Sixties, I lived in many cities in America: in New Haven, Williamstown, and in Boston; and in the South, in Durham, North Carolina; in Bloomington, Indiana, and in Austin, Texas. In those cities and towns, in America, not many people got up to offer any black person their seat. I lived through the years of the determination of that black woman, Rosa Parks, who refused to surrender her seat in the "white section" of a bus in Selma, Alabama. Not being in blackface or in anybody's face back then, I chose to sit, voluntarily, in the "black section."

Here in Toronto in those self-same Sixties, I was crossing Hoskin Avenue from Trinity College and I was wearing the College's soccer colours and I took up my position as centre forward. I did not score a goal; but I was called "off-side" three times during the match; and when the final whistle was blown, and the game was over on the Front Campus pasture, I wallowed in the cheers of the cheerleaders chosen from the beautiful first-year women students; and I headed back to Trinity College with victory in my muscles and in my loins, to the dining room at the college; and as a new resident in the college, halfway to my new home, I turned right instead of left, and after I reached Yonge Street, that was the name on the telephone pole, I guessed that I had made the wrong turn. I corrected that and turned right but it was long after the last plate of white fish and mashed potatoes in a white thin sauce had been served and eaten in the dining hall that I realized that I was lost. I began in this town by being lost, standing at the corner of Bloor and Yonge in my football uniform.

And here I am, fifty-nine years later on this same corner on a cold November evening peeling back the
years ever further than Trinity College to a time still in
Barbados when I was strong enough to run four races
– the 100 yards, the 220 yards, the 440 yards and the
880 yards – and the long jump, in one afternoon and
come first in each and then to be crowned "Victor Lud-
orum," Champion of the Games, who now finds himself
on Bloor Street, meeting himself face to Kiwi face, in the
show window of a specialty men's clothing store, Harry
Rosen's, and I find it natural to think of T.S. Eliot who
we studied during those school days and what he said
about trousers and old men:

> *I grow old… I grow old…*
> *I shall wear the bottoms of my trousers rolled.*
> *Shall I part my hair behind? Do I dare to eat a peach?*

I ate two peaches this morning. A ladies' magazine had
told me that peaches would lengthen my life but they are
my favourite fruit anyway. I like the sweet sensual tickle
of hairs kissing my mouth, but now I have to wonder
what Eliot's caution meant and still means, the way we
look so eagerly, with such yearning, for our future before
we have even got a decent look at our present, this present where in blackface I eat a peach and wear my

trousers rolled and mount a stair hoping to see a face above the stair, hoping for fairness if not friendliness, as I did back in my college days, when I stood at the top of a stairs on a stoop in a complete silence, hearing the creaking of startled shoes; the heavy sound of a dead lock, as I managed to read a well-written notice, not much larger than a tea-time calling card, stuck with Scotch tape to the inside pane of glass in the heavy, grand mahogany double door: NO COLOREDS.

On the door itself, written in an uneven hand, the assertion, or the wish: JESUS BLESS THIS HOME.

Having come through such disappointments, having lived through flushes of, if not constant, anger and disdain for more than fifty years, having taken my place on the back of the bus and then gracefully accepted my place at the front, I have witnessed my share of deterioration of the spirit, of the body. I have seen deterioration and disintegration not only in other men, those dark pouches of disappointment beneath the eyes that they blame on their livers, but increasing fragility, as a stake in itself, a fragility in my leg, my leg like life itself, covered by an infestation of scabs. And scabs that hatch. And the bone seen peeping through the flesh. And the flesh has become paper beneath my grey trousers that are loose and baggy, three sizes too large for my body, my shrunken body. It is an act of faith, this determination to stay alive while we watch ourselves shrink, doing my best, as an act of the denial of death and dying by assertively wearing my paisley scarf that catches the sunlight of the mid-afternoon, brown, grey, maroon, gold dots, commas in the design of this scarf, a silk scarf glorious and aristocratic, which is still easy for me, for I used to be a man who was studied in the taking of time, even in my years of schooling, to arrive at an aristocratic bearing; for I always wore for public appearances charcoal grey trousers with an almost indiscernible thin vertical stripe in them; a white shirt with the front stiffened by starch, and a very hot iron, a white shirt worn in dress attire with mother-of-pearl studs; and a black silk jacket, single-breasted, custom-made, in a conservative English cut, being a practising gentleman of letters, of which I knew there were and are none too many in our time, bedecking myself in such an outfit and variations of it to assert the relishing of this aristocratic self, which makes me now feel the full weight of my bladder upon me, feel the apprehension of wetness, the apprehension of the stench of pure pee and the loss of all such earned dignity as I have, earned in the deepest sense, as one earns day to day a living. I shift from foot to foot, trying to take the weight off my bladder, which suddenly has the weight of all my past years, while at the same time I try to tighten my legs, to tense my whole body, to tense my mind, try to think of elsewhere; I go over the alphabet, from A to ZED... from A to ZEE... refusing to surrender to my body, to fragility, refusing incontinence, refusing to give in to any sign that all is lost, trying to remember so simple a thing as balance, the perfect balance that accrues to being young, along, of course, with the unknowingness that also accrues to being young; but now, being old, being one of *de old folks*, no matter where I rest or reside I have lost nearly all sense of balance, have lost my focus, lost even the quickness of the eye required to read the number on my house from inside a moving taxi, that number that I myself screwed into my green-painted front door, emerald green so I can alert some driver who has picked me up, who cannot speak my language, to the fact that We are Here, I am Here! "Here-here!" Home! As I shout, "Green," and we keep going, passing by the door, having to stop and back up, being fortunate for me that there is only one door on this street that is painted green, such taxi drivers telling me, "You? Sure? Okay? If you know where it is you going…"

The last time the driver letting me out to stand on the sidewalk like a lord, a landlord, outside my own door as I revised the muddle of my thoughts by revisiting the number of steps up the staircase inside the house that climbs from the front door, up… up… up… up… up… up… up… up… up… up… up… up… up… thirteen steps… an unlucky number!… and at the first floor top step turn right; and up… and I do this each time that I return home; and I wonder if the young woman who offered me her seat climbs an exact number of steps to reach her bedroom every night? High-stepping. I am tormented by yearned-for memories of my own high-stepping, tormented because everything remembered that gives me pleasure also becomes a torment to this black man who I admit is myself, absurd in blackface, toying with the metal wing opener to his Kiwi can, who only wants, when all is said and done, to sit for an hour in a large single bathtub, to soak, in hot suds, in contentment, in comfort and ease of heart, a heart that is beating hard, having climbed another fourteen steps, having gone round a corner in a hallway in order to get to my third-floor bedroom; and although the bones in my knees do not creak and crack, I am aware that so much time is passing so quickly; each stair reminding me of time, a step, a stair, an inch gained, an inch lost; all things being equal, I like my stairs. These stairs are my country. My country for an old man. I like the dignity that comes from having had the will to set my body straight, in an erect posture, if only for a moment, in order to climb…

To where I lie on my back on my bed; and I make myself raise each leg; and count to thirty, for each leg, and I huff and puff during these calisthenics that I've come to believe in as being good for me, and then my legs plop down on the bed, a remembrance of when I ran four races, meanwhile forgetting where my cell-phone is so's to call in case of emergency alone so high up in my house… But even so, if I had my cellular phone, all the names in my pocket diary are the names of friends dead, or nearly all of them dead. Dark casualties:

"… and Tom? Whu' happen to Tom?"

"He dead."

"… and when last you see Dick?"

"Dick gone, too."

"That is life. That is the life bequeath to all o' we."

"To all o' we!"

"I hate like arse getting old…"

"Who-else dead? One foot in the grave…?"

I dial a number, and a deep-throated hum, a mis-played bass note on an organ, takes over…

"… the number you have dialled, is no longer in service."

But I am still here, yes, still in service; and glad to be, even if I am *way down upon the ribber* in this land of the living where I one day lately, on a whim, went searching through old letters and older pocket diaries determined to seek out evidence of the living, to seek out all those still whinnying with us, their names in alphabetical order, the names of men and women with whom I grew up and also men and women in this alien country of silent people who do not open their front windows and say, "Mawnin, neighbour!" And so, as if the day I did this seeking out of names was actually the Day of Dead Souls, Ash Wednesday, I called their names, one-by-one.

Down upon a river, up a creek they came, to let me mark the foreheads of my friends as each appeared before me in my bathroom mirror. I marked their brows with a penitential thumb smear of Kiwi black polish: Grace Sin-Hill. Dalton Guiler. Superintendent Boyce. Mewreel Sealey. Judy Thomas. Rudolph Hinds… I remember him, one of the best of tenors in Barbados. D. Parris. Everton Weekes (now Sir Everton Weekes). Richie Haynes (now Sir Richard Haynes). Jill Shephard. Bruce LaPorte, former Director of Black Studies at Yale University, Edward Cumberbatch, one of the best half-milers on the island, during my time, running on a hot afternoon track, marked in staggered lanes… and Malcolm X, Roy McMurtry (Judge of the Supreme Court), Norman Mailer, Morley, wagging his cane at me, telling me, "First, you outlive the bastards, then you out-write them"… all such as these rising up in my mirror full of pride but marked by penitence, standing in their youth like standing in a river to surrender their seats to me, singing along with me, *dere's whu de old folks stay*, and among them, many beautiful women. Yes, beautiful. Surrendering. Yes, but on what grounds was this surrender made in my favour? Grounds that made me and still make me suspicious. Why does this unalloyed kindness bring out in me such suspicion?

It is the raw suspicion that I am a mere hindrance, to be helped as a way of avoidance, a suspicion that I do not

seem to be an elderly, well-dressed West Indian gentleman… "an older man," a phrase used and regarded as a
term of dignity and respect back in Barbados but here, in
Toronto, there is no doff of the hat, no pleasant smile on
the face, no wave of the hand. Suspicion that here in this
country, in the privacy of the heart, I am regarded as "an
old piece o' shit!" as my feet stumble and slip and slide
on the moving steps of an escalator, or, upon my walking
into a revolving door, being caught in the door by the
rude disregard of the person ahead of me, so that, given
the cautiousness common to old men, I freeze and
become stiff, and I look as if I am dead – a corpse in a
revolving door – and I go round two times more, against
my will, sometimes three more carousel times!… before
I dare to slip out and disappear in a silence of self-accu-
sation and shame, completely bewildered as I hear from
a distance the lazy lapping of waves at the edge of a
beach where there is the smell of saltiness after a wave
has died and the soft whisper of that dying breath
touches my own lips with the fire of an unexpected kiss.
A kiss that tells me that I love life. I love life even as I
embrace wishes of the way I would like to die, to die in
my sleep, in the embrace of sleep, where I would be
insensitive to what is going on around me… But in the
meantime… it is this "meantime" my God, that kills me.
This meantime state of slow-moving uselessness like a
sudden slap of blindness, this meantime in which so it

seems I am having to re-learn, like a child, all the things I have taken for granted, that I take for granted on Bloor Street on this damp November Saturday late afternoon when I look up warily to see who is walking directly in my path and I pick a man, with my warning antennae out of the strolling crowd. He too is slow. He too is shaking. He tries to control two walking sticks. They wobble as he walks. He's hardly walking. Shuffling and stumbling. He raises the walking stick in his left hand, to greet me. Something like crazed glee, huge relief in his eye at seeing me. Certainly I recognize the man. But I do not understand why, of all the people to slip in and out of my memory, I should be confronted by this man. The stick in his left hand waves. I do not know if this is enthusiasm. Or threat. "Dave, short for Davenport. My name is Davenport. Windsor-hyphen-Britain." Dave! Oh God, oh God! From Trinidad. We were at U of T together. 1955. The stick in his right hand joins the other stick, waving his greeting. I pretend I do not recognize him. I am in blackface. Shining face. Shining with youngness. Doing my imitation of Al Jolson. He stops in my path. He is smiling. He is happy to see me. He is blocking me. I read his happiness at meeting his old friend. But I move around him. Out of his path. *My heart is turning ebber.* His mouth is open. I raise my right arm and say, like I used to in those civil right days, "Do you know what time it is?" His mouth hangs more open.

I have spotted a taxi. The taxi stops. "Where you going, old man?" the taxi driver calls out to me in a foreign accent, leaning across the front seat. I guess he is from Somalia. Or Nigeria. Or Niger. Or Zimbabwe. Or another country in Africa where they held the slaves before they packed them into small holds. Before they were shipped out on the passage to America and the West Indies.

Immediately, I resent this African, calling me an old man, when I am trying to cut years off my life; in protest against girls and women who offer me their seats on crowded buses, and in the subway; and in long lineups; and such meetings as this, meeting up, unsuspecting, with old lost friends, who, immediately in their flesh, in their deterioration held up by two walking sticks, remind me of how inevitably and finally lost I am. *Swanee*, I tell the driver. Take me to Swanee.

AUSTIN CLARKE:
RIDING THE COLTRANE

by Barry Callaghan

I walked up to the Big Man's house, and I call him Big
Man not because he is burly but because he has presence, he knows who he is, an island man who's ended up
inland, a sunshine man who has ended up in snow country. He's got an air of stillness about him, a quiet easeful-
ness, the public stance, I suspect, of a man who has
learned how to control private terrors. For forty years, I
have watched how self-contained he is, how relentlessly
calm. I contemplate his calm as he contemplates me. In
silence. We have the gift of silence. Neither of us has the
need to impinge or impose. Not on each other. We don't
need to talk, though we can both talk your ear off at the
drop of a hat. Neither of us wears a hat. Hatless, we feel
free to say anything we want to say but because we are
free, we are free to have nothing to say.

He's a decorous man, a donnish man who likes to take
a pew at high mass on Sunday at the Anglican cathedral,
and he likes to take a chair at high table at Trinity
College, but he has always lived downtown, close to low
life, to pimps, moochers, and drug peddlers, elbow to

elbow with the street action, where he can watch how the police *do* behave and misbehave. But, for all that, low life has never laid a glove on him, not on his style. If this were 1920 he would be wearing spats and puttees. A touch Edwardian. He certainly would be sporting a Homburg hat. But it's now. Linen jackets and penny loafers are stylish. Wig hats and po'-boy cotton picker coveralls are hip. He is too cool to be stylish or hip.

Sometimes he dresses like a cricketer, a white sweater with a maroon band at the V-neck. But he doesn't play cricket and no one he knows in his town plays cricket. Often, he shows up in a tweed jacket of an Oxford Street cut, but Oxford Street is not his alley, and for chandelier-lit suppers, he will appear in black tie – though black tie has not been called for. At one such supper, while in a tuxedo, he also wore a tiny headset. He was listening on the radio to a Blue Jays baseball game. As an elegant woman from Rome at his elbow talked on, he relaxed his paunch and fell asleep. He remembers dozing: "Dozing off is my habit, while reading, while drinking, while eating. And once, when I was a much younger man, a woman accused me to my face of dozing off while making love when she was on the brink of orgasm. I left her with no satisfaction. I do not remember her name." He does not remember the woman from Rome but he remembers sitting straight up at the supper table. As if attentive. A trick he learned at Combermere School for

Boys on that bump of land in the sea called Barbados. It is his home that isn't his home: the place where he was expected to grow up stupid under the Union Jack but instead he grew up smart. Maybe that is why he dresses like he's from somewhere else. He's always been from somewhere else, even in his own family, where he was the illegitimate child, cherished, but illegitimate, in a country house.

When he laughs he laughs best when he talks country. He talks country when he gets ready to cook country – ox tails and breadfruit cou cou. "Get a fair-size breadfruit, with the stem still in; and wash-she-off; and cut-she-up in eight pieces; peel-off the skin. The skin gotta be turning almost yellow. Put she in a skillet o' cold water, enough to cover-over the breadfruit; and before you cover-she down, sprinkle a lil salt over she."

Before you cover-he down you'll soon discover that the Big Man also loves *café noir* style – bop till you drop carrying on – Malpeque oysters and dry martinis in a long-stemmed glass (two olives), and rib-eye steak at Bigliardi's Off-Track Champions Betting Bar where, after making a modest wager on a pony, he will put on his intellectual spats and try to explain how Derek Walcott – being a black poet talking to black writers like himself – has "faced the insistent question of our schizophrenia... faced the question, and recognized that it is our schizophrenia, in fact, that have given us (as blacks) our most positive definition." It is true: though, of course, he is not clinically schizophrenic, Clarke does answer – 'pon the call – to two names, Austin & Tom, and he easily gets lost, caught – betwixt and between.[1]

On this day, Austin tells me Tom is cooking – and he is stern about it – Tom *is* cooking and he *is* cooking island "food that'll bring on the bess spiritual unctuousness and grace," and he expects me to be at his house because, among others, his old friend, the Chief Justice of the Supreme Court, is going to amble on through the side-street downtown hookers and druggies, and the Mister Chief Justice – in Clarke's house – is going to partake of pigs feet and punkin, squash and christophenes.

"The feed bag is on."

When he say the feed bag is on is not a time to *foop* with the man in his house.

It is a writer's house behind a wrought-iron gate, except for the big flag over the door (a red maple leaf FLAG: I can't ever get used to writers anywhere who FLAG their patriotism). The small rooms, made cozy by a certain clutter, smell of pipe tobacco: Amphora, Mixture 79. There are books on the chairs, books on the

---

[1] He also answers to the call of being the author of nine novels and six short-story collections, most notably *The Polished Hoe*, winner of the 2002 Giller Prize, the 2003 Commonwealth Writers' Prize, and the 16th annual Trillium Prize.

floor, papers on the sofa and books on the papers. Where did he sit Malcolm X when the X-man came to see him? And all the visitin' Wessindian diplomats and the local Conservative Party honchos (Big Man, the *foop* man, is a Tory), and Salome Bey the singer and Harry Somers the composer, and what about Norman Mailer? Did he walk Mailer through the house?

There are books, tread on tread, up the narrow stairs.

On the second floor, there is his writing room, and his bedroom, too, with a large black-and-white portrait of Billie Holiday overseeing the bed, a wrought-iron and seemingly fragile bed on tall legs, a princely barque, afloat, "high high, pon which a man or woman would have to jump up and then jump down." Most of the time when I ask him what's happening and how he is doing he says – looking grey under the eyes – that he hasn't slept for three days, being hunkered over his keyboard, writing, trying to find "the right word pon the page," and in trying to do so, he says he also hasn't eaten for three days. He grows curiouser and curiouser – he dozes off in public but doesn't seem to sleep at home, and though he loves to cook, he often goes without food, and though he is a man of prose he quotes poetry about being betwixt and between.

> ... *how choose*
> *Between this African and the English tongue I love?*

Betray them both, or give back what they give?
How can I face this slaughter and be cool?

In his kitchen he is wild in his airs of decorum: immaculate white shirt, a striped tie of a darker sensible hue, and his good old tweed jacket of the Oxford Street cut. Bending over a burning stove, stirring pots with a long wooden spoon, talking to me about the food he "does make," he is hassled in his head because he does not have the exact "ingreasements," so that his beans and rice will taste "good good pon a fork, if you are fussy."

He is dressed as uptown Austin but he is talking down home Tom, his Bajan voice, for it is Tom Clarke that they call him in Barbados, Tom – who writes a column in the newspaper and tells his readers, "Don't lissen to no foolishness, particular the kinds and the res and talk emanating from the mouths of neither preachers nor priests; neither vicar nor dean; canon nor bishop; neither lord bishop nor archbishop; nor none-so. Lissen to the gamblers, first. And then, nod-off."

Mind you, when he was Tom, the barefoot boy in Barbados, he did no nodding, he *was* a *blur*. As Tom, the teenager, he ran the 100 yards in 10 flat, an island record that Austin says still stands. But now, be it Tom or Austin, he's an over-the-hill athlete with a slight paunch. We share that: old jocks, and I assure Austin that as a basketball player I was sneaky-fast, change-of-pace fast, but Tom smiles, knowing he would have left me in his dust, 10-flat. My only consolation is that Tom might have been fast then but Austin is now the slowest man I know, as slow moving as his stirring of the foods in his pots, ponderously slow so that they won't get bun bun (burnt!), and he tells me to drink up my long-stemmed martini, and get myself ready to get full-up, but also *mos important* – to expect no dessert – no dessert because dessert is not eaten by Wessindians unless the meal is so light in its offerings and you need "to full-up everybody's belly."

There are no light offerings in Austin's house. He's got deep pockets, even when he's broke, and his generosity is often profligate in direct relation to his debts – and so, smiling upon self-indulgence, he fires up another martini for me. The Big Man – cooking cou cou as he dreams up new fictions to tell old hard truths, as he waits for his Tory pal, the affable Supreme Court judge, to come for a meal of port and lima beans – he stirs his pot, and turns *up* the silver knobs to his sound system, the sound of which is John Coltrane, the Trane's tenor horn, and it occurs to me that this is where Tom and Austin meet, over a pot of cou cou, smack-dab in Coltrane.

Like a Coltrane chorus, Clarke's paragraphs – as he sits writing bare-assed in the midnight hours before his computer – don't really begin, they just start, they don't end, they stop. He does not surrender the paragraph form (just as Coltrane did not surrender the 12-bar blues grid): but both perform as if form were a jail cell and a chorus is a jailbreak[2]: within the form there are dissonances, counter notes, divided meters (a study could be done of Clarke's discordant placing of semicolons), and the extended lyric runs that sometimes invert and always imply the melody – the storyline – while seeming to wreck it, a lyrical vexation if not outright anger – modulated to a sweetness:

> ... and in that time, it was he who understood that a little mistake, a word said under the breath but loud enough for Mas'r to hear; the misappropriation of one of those freed hens in the yards; the miscalculation in the pouring of molasses for the horse and jackass, leaving too deep a bottom in the bottom of the pail; and his ignorance of mathematics and addition, but his proficiency with subtraction: twenty hams was put in the smoke-filled shed with the hickory leaves and the smoke broke out as if the whole goddamn place was on fire, Mas'r; and he said, under his breath, but too loud, Amma wish this goddamn place were going up in flame with these hams; but when he checked their smoking and their curing, one was gone. One gone! These two words became like a bell in the

---

[2] Clarke's friend, the painter Harold Towne, used to speak of form as "the tyranny of the corner." He painted against the corner as Clarke writes against the paragraph.

night, like a boot at the door, like a tap on the shoulder in a crowd, like the leather in the boot of the Gestapo, all over that land across the body of water. "One gone!" And dogs barked. Lights came on. Lanterns were carried. Dogs yelped, tasting the sweetness of blood. Whips were cracked for suppleness. And for length. And for deadliness. And men jumped on the backs of horses. Rifles and pistols were taken from their shelves, already oiled and ready for use. Bullets and shots were fired for practice in the air. And the small children, who knew those two words, laughed in their sleep, and wished, and wished.

The prose line has been sprung for suppleness.

The ingreasements are semicoloned.

The doorbell rang.

I'm sure the FLAG stood to attention.

I stepped out of the kitchen – out of (I thought) the music – into the tiny fenced-in downtown backyard. The air circuits were wired. Speakers were stationed at the foot of the back walls of the house: ghetto-blasting speakers: indifferent to decorum, the don was not only putting on a feed, he was pumping out Coltrane – he was *churching* the neighbourhood… searing jolts of sweet tenor sax and bass clarinet, so loud it could not be ignored by anyone in the near distance, certainly not by the neighbours, and not even by a nocturnal raccoon, an old night prowler who had come down out of its sugar maple tree 'to sit – with minstrel-shoe eyes – on the fence, betwixt and between yards. It stared at me. I stared at it. Absolutely calm. A silence. Except for Trane's horn spiralling around McCoy Tyner's triplets; they were playing "Soul Eyes." The Big Man had willfully changed the feel in the air of the whole downtown block, in a 10-flat *blur*. Coltrane was in B-flat. And Clarke was standing in the backdoor of the house, the big heavy-set judge on his arm, the judge flushed from his display of goodwill, the two of them beamish, two high Anglican dignitaries, and their legitimacy – like their friendship – was beyond question. I realized there could be no recipe for knowing who Austin is, but only a consideration of his ingreasements.

Austin Clarke
by David Annesley

AUSTIN CLARKE

THERE ARE NO
ELDERS

INTRODUCTION BY LEON ROOKE

EXILE CLASSICS • NUMBER FIVE
with material for book clubs and classrooms

Available from Exile Editions

AUSTIN CLARKE

IN THIS CITY

INTRODUCTION BY DAVID CHARIANDY

EXILE CLASSICS • NUMBER TEN
with material for book clubs and classrooms

www.ExileEditions.com

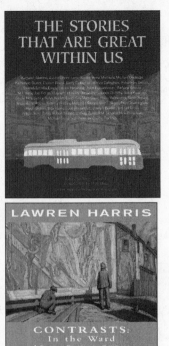

THE STORIES THAT ARE GREAT WITHIN US

432 pages with over 50 contributors, including Margaret Atwood, Leon Rooke, Anne Michaels, Michael Ondaatje, Katherine Govier, Dionne Brand, Austin Clarke, Barry Callaghan, Morley Callaghan, Robertson Davies, Steven Hayward, Gwendolyn MacEwen, Barbara Gowdy, M.T. Kelly… and artists Michael Snow, Sorel Etrog, Robert Markle, R.M. Schafer and Charlie Pachter.

LAWREN HARRIS CONTRASTS

Group of Seven painter Lawren Harris' poetry and paintings take the reader on a unique historical journey that offers a glimpse of our country's past as it was during early urbanization. 168 pages, with 16 colour paintings by Harris. Introduction and Walking Tour by Gregory Betts.

YIDDISH WOMEN WRITERS

Major anthologies of Yiddish prose in translation concentrate on popular male writers. This is a unique 306-page anthology of short stories, and excerpts from novels and memoirs, that features 13 women of literary distinction.

THE SECOND

An erudite work of fiction in which characters clash over the complex ideologies that shape politics, religion, and spirituality, ultimately confronting their individual identities through the realization of just how hard it is to make belief believable. 580 pages.

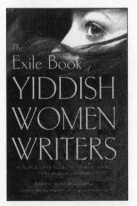

EXILE
e d i t i o n s
Fiction, Poetry, Translation, Drama and Nonfiction

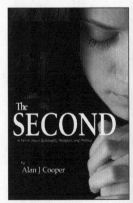

2013 RELEASES

DEAD NORTH: CANADIAN ZOMBIE FICTION

An enjoyable and rollicking ride, this collection of Canadian Zombie Fiction contains 20 stories exploring a broad spectrum of the undead, from Romero-style corpses to those inspired by Aboriginal mythology, all shambling against the background of the Great White North.

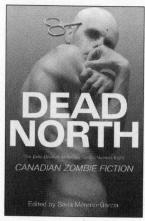

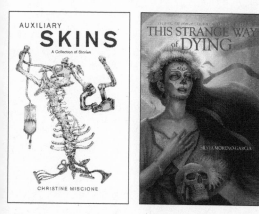

AUXILIARY SKINS

This writer's laboratory reveals life in a way to turn the reader's imagination loose. Christine Miscione's debut collection illumines all that's perilous, beautiful and raw about being human. From the surgically gutted, to the racially transformed, to a story of self-excision that won year two of Exile's $15,000 Short Fiction Competition, this collection is chock-full of razor blades masquerading as lemon tarts and everything in between.

THIS STRANGE WAY OF DYING

Spanning a variety of genres – fantasy, science fiction, horror – and time periods, Silvia Moreno-Garcia's debut collection features short stories infused with Mexican folklore yet firmly rooted in a reality that transforms as the fantastic erodes the rational. Moreno-Garcia was year-one winner of Exile's $15,000 Short Fiction Competition.

Available from Exile Editions or Amazon
www.ExileEditions.com

$15,000 Short Fiction Competition

AUSTIN CLARKE has won the Giller, Commonwealth, Trillium, and Writers' Trust awards ~ in 2013 he shared the $5,000 prize in Exile's $15,000 Short Fiction Competition.

$10,000 best story by an emerging writer

$5,000 best story by a writer at any career point

The 12 shortlisted are published in the annual *CVC Short Fiction Anthology* series, and *ELQ/Exile: the Literary Quarterly*

**Both competitions open in October
guidelines/forms at www.TheExileWriters.com**

CVC Anthology One: Frank Westcott, Richard Van Camp, Gregory Betts, Kristi-Ly Green, Rishma Dunlop, Zoe Stikeman, Silvia Moreno-Garcia, Leigh Nash, Hugh Graham, Ken Stange

CVC Anthology Two: Christine Miscione, Leon Rooke, Kelly Watt, Darlene Madott, Linda Rogers, Daniel Perry, Amy Stuart, Phil Della, Jacqueline Windh, Kris Bertin, Martha Bátiz, Seán Virgo

CVC Anthology Three: Sang Kim, George McWhirter, David Somers, Leon Rooke, Helen Marshall, Priscila Uppal, Yakos Spiliotopoulos, Greg Hollingshead, Matthew R. Loney, Rob Peters, Liz Windhorst Harmer, Austin Clarke

Purchase the CVC Anthologies at www.ExileEditions.com or Amazon

$2,500 Poetry Competition

$2,000 for the best suite of poetry

$500 for the best poem

Winners are published in *ELQ/Exile: the Literary Quarterly*